The Home of Best Modern Pulp Fiction

The Magazine of

Unbelievable Stories

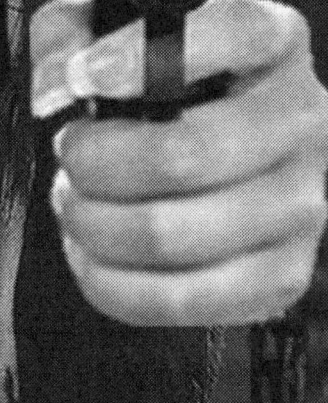

The Harridan
Is she Dr. Royce's dream or worst nightmare?

Warriors of The Sun
Will humans survive the end of the world?

Searching For Love
Can Sassy get the love potion to work on the man she wants to have?

April 2007
Vol II No 1

Don't miss Ghost PI, Space Adventure, & Time Travel Story

QPN Press
Yucaipa, CA 92399
www.quill-pen.net

ISBN 978-0-6151-4161-9

The Magazine of
Unbelievable Stories
April 2007 VOL II No 1

Andrei V. Lefebvre, Publisher

Christina Barber, Editor
Horror, End of the World

Cheryl Wright, Editor
Romance

Darlene Oakley, Editor
Space Opera & Time Travel

Elysabeth Eldering, Editor
Paranormal Mystery

The contact information is as follows:
avl@quill-pen.net

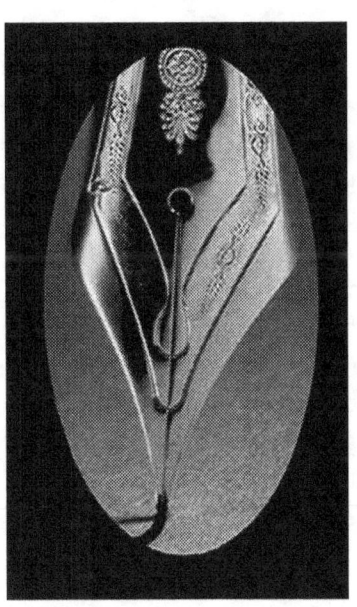

From the Publisher

Dear Friends,

Thank you for picking up the April copy of The Magazine of Unbelievable Stories. This is the first issue of four for the 2007 run. This year we changed the format somewhat. Here, you will find the first installments for the six new series.

Our Horror Editor Christina Barber came up with a storyline about a doctor to the horror creatures. H.F. Gibbard answered her call for submissions and penned a great story. His is a tale of lust, greed, and idealism. Don't miss it!

If you enjoy paranormal mysteries, the Renegade Angel storyline—created by Mystery Editor Elysabeth Eldering—is for you. Batya Deene created a tale of suspense and drama which will keep your eyes glued to the pages.

No self-respecting pulp fiction book can do without romance. Our Editor Cheryl Wright conjured up a series about a contemporary young woman in Searching for Love. Heidi Kneale wrote a story with an unusual twist on a love potion subject. What imagination!

We couldn't do without space adventure either. Darlene Oakley, our Space Travel Editor, created a series appropriately named Space Opera. Margreta Eubanks wrote a story about a deep space intrigue and adventure. Awesome!

What if our civilization—as we know it today—would have disappeared in a flash? Well, then we would have had no choice but to enter the realm of Christina Barber's series titled Warriors of the Sun. Susan Brundige used her talent to write a great first installment for it. Mad Max move over, the new champ is in town.

We also have a time travel story in this issue (and you thought we would forget). The series is a brainchild of Darlene Oakley who named it To Save Pearl. Jennifer DiCamillo wrote an intriguing back-to-the-past tale worth your undivided attention. Great ending!

Thank you again and enjoy the stories!

Andrei V. Lefebvre
Publisher

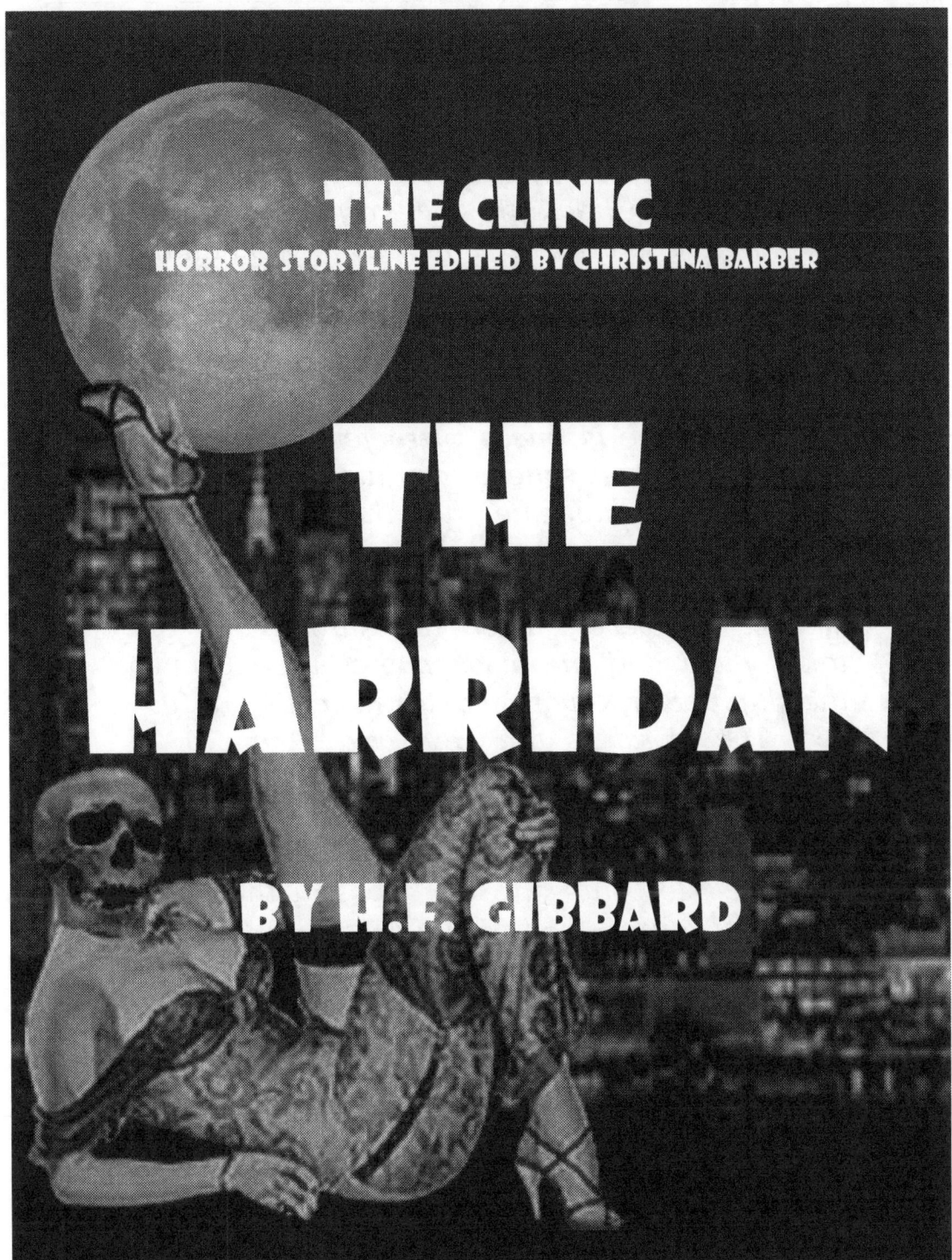

THE CLINIC
HORROR STORYLINE EDITED BY CHRISTINA BARBER

THE HARRIDAN

BY H.F. GIBBARD

Dear Readers,

Dr. Brandon Royce runs a very special clinic, one that heals the sick, dying or insane. His specialty is what sets him apart from all the other doctors. His clients are supernatural - beasts that prowl the night - vampires, lycanthropes, ghouls, demons, gargoyles and the like.

Dr. Royce is one of very few humans 'in the know' about these creatures. Most of humanity has no clue that they exist, living right here, among the population.

By day Doctor Royce sleeps, as do his clients. However, when the shroud of night takes flight and the moon makes its ascent to the sky, Doctor Royce resumes his call of duty.

The world is the here and now (2007). When the sun sets, the world changes dramatically, catering to those that lurk in the dark shadows of the night.

We step into the darkness with Doctor Brandon Royce – just another usual night with a packed waiting room brought about by a full moon.

Enjoy your first thrilling ride to the Clinic with 'The Harridan' by HF Gibbard!

Christina Barber
Horror Editor

The Harridan

I was shoveling down my take-out Szechuan chicken from a little all-night place on 42nd Street when I heard the scream. It came down the hall, from the waiting room out front. I tossed my chopsticks onto a stainless steel tray. It took me a second to jerk on my lab coat, to check the mirror, straighten my glasses, and run my fingers through my hair. Then I began jogging down the hall, my keys jingling against the pager in my pocket.

A second scream came down the hall, louder than the first. Glenda stuck her head into the hallway.

"Glenda, you and Mavis to the waiting room!" I called to her, "Stat!"

I caught a quick glimpse behind Glenda of Mr. Tedescu, hooked up to a transfusion bag. He was one of four we had on transfusion tonight. The aging vampire blinked and gave me a perplexed look as I jogged by.

I knew what was waiting for me out in front. I'd heard the cry of the Harridan before. It's not something you tend to forget.

The Harridan was naked. I hadn't anticipated that. It stopped me for a minute, like I'd hit a brick wall.

Two uniformed cops had hold of her writhing, extended arms, one on each arm. A broken set of handcuffs jingled from her wrists. The cops cursed, struggling to keep her long red nails out of their eyes. Her hands were crimson with blood. She howled an animal cry and twisted her head around, trying to bite them with her reddened teeth.

The Harridan struggled to escape. Her pelvis gyrated wildly. Her perfectly-formed breasts heaved to and fro. Every inch of her tanned and smoothly muscled body was moving, sweating, twisting, thrusting . . .the gyrations made me snap involuntarily to attention, creating a bulge in my pants that I could only hope was hidden by my lab coat.

Her face, twisted with rage, was unspeakably beautiful. Her long, scarlet hair whipped over her shoulders with each compulsive jerk of her head. I saw that her abdomen was covered in blood. Not her own. The blood reminded me what she--what it--really was.

Then Glenda and Mavis entered the room, breaking my trance. They headed straight for the Harridan.

Glenda looked unfazed as she brushed past me. Her starched uniform barely fit around her muscled shoulders. Baby linebacker, she called herself.

Glenda grabbed hold of one of the Harridan's legs in her greenish hands, lifted it, and twisted it, giving me a view that no amount of medical training could have prepared me for. Mavis waded in with a syringe, and injected the Harridan inside her smooth, tanned thigh.

The Harridan gave a little moan, one that made the hair on my neck rise.

Then she collapsed to the floor.

"So, what's the story, Officer, uh--" I checked the obese cop's badge. "Malley?"

Glenda and Mavis worked efficiently to trundle the Harridan onto a stretcher. I tried to keep my attention on Officer Malley. It wasn't easy.

"Her name's Aesha," Malley said, wiping sweat from his forehead, "One of Gargonzola's girlfriends."

Jimmy Gargonzola. Figures. That little hood was a six-pack of trouble. He still owed me, for getting a Golem off his tail a while back.

"She messed up a customer. Really bad. He's in the hospital now. Might not make it."

A customer! Jimmy was more of a fool than I thought. You don't pimp a Harridan. Not if you want the John to come back in one piece. And especially not on a night like tonight, with the full moon blazing silver, beating down on every night creature that strolls the streets, driving them crazy with hunger.

Granted, a Harridan would give a guy a night to remember, an experience of sheer copulatory pleasure that would make any real woman seem tame by comparison. For dessert, though, she would split that lucky guy stem to stern and eat his guts out. A Harridan, you see, is a predator, a thing that does a perfect imitation of a beautiful woman to ensnare its prey. Just like those undersea mud creatures that dangle pretty bits of fake seaweed in front of the little fishies, then snap them up when they take the bait.

Mr. Tedescu walked slowly through the waiting room, leaning on his cane, heading for the front desk. He'd need another transfusion, two weeks from now. Judy, my receptionist, nodded, put down her emery board, and clacked some keys on the computer.

"Good night, Todor," I called to him.

Tedescu turned and looked at me, then the cop. He lifted his hat and bowed with a flourish. "Yes," he said, straightening up and giving me a toothy smile, with just a touch of Rumanian lilt in his voice, "Yes, it is a good night. A good night, indeed. I feel quite refreshed, Doctor Royce."

He wasn't fooling anybody. Himself or me. I saw the droopy fangs, the lines around his mouth. Todor was dying. Dying of VARAS, Vampire-Related Accelerated Aging Syndrome. The chilling new disease, cause as yet unknown.

Todor couldn't even hunt up his own food anymore. It would be time to line up hospice care for him soon.

I've seen vamps die before, of old age. They don't live forever, you know, just a hell of a long time. Their cellular clock runs on a slower timetable than yours or mine.

They hate the thought of cremation. They want to be shipped back to the old country for burial. Usually, though, it takes them hundreds of years to fade away. Todor wasn't a day over eighty. Thinking about that, seeing him like this, broke me up inside.

"Jimmy wants you to keep her under wraps for a while," Officer Malley said, "until things blow over."

I turned back to the cop and looked him straight in the eye. Malley was on the mob payroll. A fact of life in this city. Still, all the bowing and scraping, the sheer deference corrupt cops like Malley give to slimy hoods like Jimmy Gargonzola has always turned my stomach.

"This is a medical clinic," I said, poking a finger toward his fat gut, "I'm not running a safe house for the mob here. I'll keep her sedated overnight, get her cleaned up. But you tell Jimmy it's not my job to hide his whores."

He shrugged. After a minute, he said, "Okay, I'll tell him." He didn't add, "it's your funeral."

* * *

Four a.m., an hour 'til quitting time, and I'd almost forgotten Mavis's party. Glenda came and got me. I had them both on the night shift tonight, doubled up, due to the full moon. The three of us crowded around the little table in the tiny break room. Disco party music played softly on a beat up cassette player up on a shelf.

There were two birthday cakes arranged on the linoleum table. They'd left the candles off mine. Good thing: it helped me tell the cakes apart. I wouldn't want to be eating what was in theirs. Not for a million bucks.

Their cake had three candles on it. One for each of the three years since Mavis's resurrection.

"Happy birthday, Mavis," I said, after she'd blown out the candles. I handed her the package I'd concealed beneath my lab coat.

She gave me a huge, toothy grin as she took the present. I saw a single tear roll out of her partially decomposed eye.

Once upon a time, before she took what she called her long dirt bath, Mavis had been a beautiful young black woman. She kept a torn, sepia-toned picture of herself in the break room, dressed like an old-time lace-frilled Victorian, twirling an umbrella. The picture was from a happier time, pre-mortem, when her whole family had gone to Nevada.

Ghouls like old photographs, which is why I knew Mavis would love her birthday present from me. I'd found it buried in the dusty bottom of a discount table at the local Barnes and Noble. Big enough to sit on somebody's coffee table. That is, if that somebody wanted to display a book entitled African-American Cemeteries, 1890 - 1930.

The ill-tended cemeteries in the book, from New Orleans to the Kansas plains, from Oklahoma to Tennessee, had been photographed in depressingly stark, high-contrast black and white. Flipping through the book, I'd seen haunting images of yellowed and dying blades of tall grass, rusted and decrepit gate hinges, desiccated and twisted tree limbs, fallen and moldering tombstones.

Mavis loved it, every page. She flipped through the book with glee in her eyes, the kind of pure joy you see in your daughter when you buy her a pony or a pair of roller skates.

"Thank you, Doctor Royce!" she called out, and threw her arms around me. "Thank you! Thank you!" The cold, loose skin of her face rubbed against my neck, making the hair stand up on my arms.

* * *

I slept hard all the next day, exhausted. My third ghoul nurse, Belinda, pulled the day shift, watching over our two inpatients.

When I came back on duty at 6:00, I went to check on Aesha first thing. The nurses had dressed her in a hospital gown and strapped her to the bed hand and foot with heavy leather restraints. She'd tuned the TV to the Home Shopping Channel. She clutched the remote in the talons of her right hand. She shot me an angry look, then caught herself and gave me a smile.

"Hello, Doctor Royce," she purred.

"You seem a little calmer tonight, Aesha," I said, "That's good."

"Yes," she said. She looked up at the TV, then back at me. Her eyes widened. "I was very naughty last night. Very, very naughty. And you saw me NAKED!"

She wriggled a little, and went on, grinning seductively. "I didn't mind that, though. I LIKE for you to see me naked." She paused a beat, then in a whispery voice she asked, "Did YOU like what you saw?"

A picture flashed into my mind, of Glenda lifting the creature's smooth and perfect leg, exposing the most hidden parts of her anatomy. I snapped to attention again. Couldn't help it. But neither could I let Aesha see the effect she had on me.

I did what I always do when I find myself with unwanted arousal.

Started thinking about Mozart. The music of Wolfgang Amadeus Mozart, to my mind, is the most un-erotic arrangement of musical notes imaginable. A form of auditory birth control. A few bars of Eine Kleine Nachtmusik running through my head, and I felt myself start to soften again.

"I've got a secret!" Aesha sang.

It suddenly came to me, while running Mozart's most famous air through my head, that a Harridan probably has no understanding whatsoever of human erotic feeling. The words Aesha said, the posturing of her body, the breathy tones she adopted, were instinctual evolutionary adaptations designed to attract her prey. Like an insect that imitates a mating call or a pheromone of another species to lure its victims to their deaths, a Harridan casts a phony and unfeeling erotic spell over its human male targets. With this revelation, and the intellectualizing that went with it, the rest of my erection disappeared.

"That's nice," I said.

She pouted. "Don't you want to know my secret?"

"That depends," I said, typing in some notes on my portable electronic keyboard.

"Depends on what?"

"Depends, my dear, on whether you are ready to behave yourself so that we can process your paperwork and get you released from this clinic."

"Released? But I want to stay here. With YOU, doctor Royce!"

"Yeah. Yeah, sure you do."

"My secret's about Bill Hathaway."

I stopped typing.

"Did you say Bill Hathaway?" I asked, looking at her carefully.

She grinned, a knowing, triumphant grin, happy to have broken through my shell. Hearing this sleazy little bottom-feeder tell me she had a secret about Bill Hathaway was the last thing I'd expected tonight. But, then, life is full of surprises.

"Jimmy was talking about him. He said there's a hit going down."

"A hit?"

"Mmm, hmm."

"On Bill?"

"Mmm, hmm."

"Why are you telling me this, Aesha?"

She sat silent for a moment, then let it fly.

"Because . . .I hate him!" Her face twisted into a mask of petulance.

"Jimmy's a little turd! He has his big mooks tie me down to the bed. Then he lets guys screw me! Not that I mind that . . ." She looked wistful for a second, then her face hardened. "But he doesn't let me FEED afterwards. It's like being force-fed, then having your stomach pumped! Then he feeds me raw cow meat, from the store, just to keep me alive!"

She was working her way up to a screaming fit now, the kind only a

Harridan can throw. Only she couldn't quite get there. The aftereffects of sedation had knocked the edge off her anger, so it was more like an extended whine.

"I don't do well on cow meat! I'm allergic! It gives me yeast infections and irritable bowel syndrome! My digestion is all screwed up! He--"

I interrupted her. "Tell me some more about Bill Hathaway. Why a hit? What's Jimmy's involvement? It makes no sense."

She ignored my question. "I showed Jimmy last night, though," she said, a wicked grin on her face, "I got loose, and I got FED!"

Just then, Glenda knocked on the partially-opened door, pushing it all the way open. She stepped into the room, a frown on her face.

"There's a Mr. Gargonzola in the waiting room to see you, doctor," she said.

Jimmy was expansive, friendly, painstakingly affable. He hugged me.

I towered over him. It was like being hugged by a kid. Except that I felt his gun holster beneath his shirt press into my chest. Then he shook my hand and squeezed my shoulder, smiling a perfect smile from ear to ear.

"I hear ya got my woman back he-ah," he says, "Tanks for watching over ha."

Mavis was undoing the leather straps when we walked in the room.

"A-yeh!" Jimmy exclaimed, giving me a wink, "Got ha flat on ha back!" In a stage whisper to me, he said, "Just how she belongs."

"Can it, Jimmy!" Aesha yelled.

"Aren't ya happy to see me, baby?" he asked.

Aesha tumbled off the bed. She hugged Jimmy and gave him a kiss.

After a second, he pushed her away.

"Easy, baby," he said, a little nervous, then smoothed his silk shirt.

Jimmy paid her bill. No insurance. He shrugged off my advice about leaving nasty pets like the Harridan out in the wild where they belong. She might seem tame now, I told him, but wait until the sedation wears off . . .

He told me he'd reached an "arrangement" with the cops and the victim's family, so Aesha could leave with him. He thanked me again, then strolled off to his limo at the curb, hand in hand with Aesha, a long coat thrown over her hospital gown. She didn't look back.

It bothered me the rest of the evening, like an itch that I couldn't quite scratch. Let's assume Aesha was telling the truth. Why would anybody want to kill Bill Hathaway? Since the Seventies, he's been the closest thing to a Mother Teresa we've got down here.

I wasn't about to call Bill. I knew how he operated. Bill was not a guy to take a mere unvarnished threat seriously.

Around midnight, I went back to my office, behind the operating room, grabbed my cell phone, and dialed up an old friend. Norman Chandler, a/k/a Stormin' Norman, was the only private security guy I knew, and probably the only security guard in the city, who could protect you from an angry spook or a vengeful goblin. Unfortunately, he told me, he was tied up right now, his resources stretched to the limit providing security for a summit meeting of witches from Romania, Latvia, Estonia and Thailand, taking place right this moment down at the Marriott.

Good luck, pal, I thought as I hung up, smiling a little, picturing him in the middle of a witches' summit. I guess this means I'll be paying a visit to Bill Hathaway myself.

I tossed the keys to the office to Glenda, and told her to cancel the rest of my appointments and to lock up at sunrise. I hit the darkened streets in my bomber jacket and my blue bandana, packing heat. A .38 special loaded with silver bullets, to be precise. For backup, I had a silver scalpel in a leather sheath strapped to my right calf. Just in case.

Maybe it's silly, a middle-aged guy like me toting a gun and a jacket and a bandana. But it's surprising, given my profession, how often I end up suiting up for action on behalf of a patient or a friend. Thirty years and forty pounds ago, you see, I was in the Marines. I went to med school after I finished my tour of duty. But I never quite shed the impression that sometimes, the road to healing lies down the barrel of a gun.

The moon that shone down on the city streets was almost bright enough to read by. I heard barking noises in the distance. Some of them canine, some not.

As I moved past the Pharmacia Munoz, closed for years now, I started getting nervous. The streets were deserted, foggy, but the night felt weighed down, heavy with a malevolent presence. More howling noises reached my ears. A shriek that might have been a cat in heat.

Bill's place was half a dozen blocks from the clinic. It was a squat brick building not far from skid row, the kind favored by micro-brewers and foreign car enthusiasts. Easy to mistake for an abandoned building. Bill kept a heavy padlock on the door. He had all the windows but one blacked out. The contents of the one un-blackened shop window illustrated his whimsical nature: old newspapers, a vintage TV with rabbit ears, a can of Tab soda, and a doll missing an eye.

Nobody from the straight world would have given Bill Hathaway's place a second glance. But if you were a vampire, or a shape-shifter, a were man or were woman (as they wanted to be called those days), a ghoul or a hobgoblin, or something that just came off somebody's lab table, and if you were in trouble, the word on the street was, go see Bill Hathaway. He'd take care of you.

As I approached the building, I saw that Bill's front door stood wide open. The heebie-jeebies tickled my spine like a facet joint injection. I'd never known Bill to leave his door just standing open to the street like that. Especially not at night.

I moved slowly, peered cautiously around the door frame, felt my fingers grasp the .38 in my pocket.

"Bill?" I called through the door.

No answer.

I walked into the cavernous, unfinished foyer that served as Bill's waiting room. My footsteps echoed in the room. I smelled mold, then the stench of the homeless and the despairing.

Over the years, with Bill's permission, graffiti artists and taggers had sprayed the enormous, bare brick walls inside his waiting room with amazingly intricate iconography of their daily life. My eyes wandered up an unrealistically pneumatic female vampire, naked from the waist up, her fangs dripping with blood, then to a red-eyed Djinn, holding a whip in one hand and a golden treasure-box in another. The centerpiece was a magnificent, enormous, spray-painted image of a decaying Gothic castle. It looked like a perverse mixture of Byronic Romanticism and a medieval Book of Hours. Its whitened towers glowed like abandoned bones in the moonlight, partially smeared from leaking water on the wall.

"Bill?" I called again, a little louder.

I walked forward, past a neat row of cheap plastic chairs, to Bill's battered desk in the center of the room. The desk was covered with paperwork. It looked like Bill had left in a hurry, too rushed to put the file away. I sat down on Bill's beat up leather chair. I couldn't help reading the typed summary at the end of one of the government forms.

"Mr. Andresz has demonstrated both past persecution, and a well-founded fear of future persecution, based on his nationality and religion. Mr. Andresz has been chased from his home, shot at, and hunted, by torch-wielding peasants and local Magyar security forces in Hungary. He reasonably fears torture and death if returned to that country. He is therefore a refugee in this country, and entitled to asylum."

I grinned a little, couldn't help myself. Only Bill would try to recast lycanthropy as an ethnic and religious issue. I silently wished him the best with the Department of Homeland Security.

Suddenly, I heard a noise out front. Could have been Bill, but I doubted it. I wasn't going to stick around to find out. I pushed away from the desk, and headed for the back door.

A pimply young were-man wearing an oversized muscle shirt met me in the alleyway, behind Hathaway's. Yellow light shone down on us from a dim fixture.

"Dr. Royce?" he asked.

I didn't know the kid, but he knew me. For just a moment, my fingers wrapped around the handle of the .38 in my pocket. Then I looked at him again, and the clinician in me took over. I ran a mental assessment on the kid. Adolescent lycanthrope, status post-metamorphosis, a rather nasty set of lacerations and contusions on the right shoulder.

"You get those in full wolf mode?" I asked, pointing to the shoulder.

He looked down at his feet. "Maybe," he said, shifting his weight uncomfortably.

"It was your first time, wasn't it?"

He said nothing. I noticed the blood on his blue jeans. His, no doubt.

"What do you need, son?" I asked.

He reached in the back pockets of his jeans, and pulled out a small, double-folded manila envelope.

"We're watching the place here," he said, his voice cracking just slightly, "Mr. Hathaway's . . . away. He told me to give this to you if you showed up here."

"Thank you," I said, and took the envelope.

He pulled out a skateboard from against the wall and quickly skated away down the alley.

"Don't be afraid of it!" I called after him, "It's normal, happens to everybody!"

Everybody like you, anyway, I thought. I wish I could have every adolescent werewolf over to the clinic just once, before the change, the first time, to explain to them what is going to happen. So many go through it all alone.

The boy turned the corner and was out of sight.

I drove home and opened the envelope in my living room. It contained a single cassette tape with the word "Royce" scrawled on it.

It seemed like ages since I'd been home during the night time hours. The grandfather clock next to my stereo chimed four A.M. I yawned.

I fitted the tape into my stereo, turned up the master volume with the remote, and made myself comfortable by wrapping my hand around a glass of scotch on my leather recliner.

There was a hiss, then Bill's voice said, "Brand. Brand, this is Bill Hathaway. I don't have long to talk. Hopefully my friend got to you by now. She was supposed to have you contact me."

My friend? Did he mean Aesha? Was she working for Hathaway?

"Brandon, we've got a big problem. Four days ago, one of my contacts in the Czech Republic gave me some news about VARAS. News that blew my doors off. I did some checking, and I was able to verify the information. Unfortunately, my inquiries were discovered by the wrong people. I have reason to believe my life is in danger because of what I know. I'm going to give this tape to a trusted friend. Hopefully, he'll find you and pass it on. Please contact me about this. You can find me Thursday at midnight, where you first met Julie. Goodbye, old friend."

"Where you first met Julie."

Thanks, old friend. I'd almost made myself forget about where I first met Julie.

Guido's was a restaurant down on the waterfront. Best shrimp and lobster in town. Run by the Cardino family for forty years.

Incredible food, incredible service, first-class everything. Until the Ukrainians muscled in two years ago. They shot the chef, four wait personnel and two customers all in one night, then burned the place down.

I met Julie there ten years ago, back when the place was still swinging, on a summer night that seemed to last forever, one of the three or four perfect nights allotted to a guy in his whole miserable existence. It was Bill who introduced us. We ate, and drank, Julie and me, and danced on the dock behind Guido's while the waves lapped the shore and the full moon caressed her bare shoulders.

It lasted three years, until she got sick of what I did for a living.

Julie taught at a deaf school. For kids. One of them didn't come home one night. The word was he was mutilated by a werewolf.

We had fights after that. Julie wanted me to go into a normal practice, on humans, in the 'burbs. I wouldn't back down. She left me the Dear John letter stuck with a borrowed scalpel to the clinic door. A traumatic gesture, typical of her.

I haven't been serious about another woman since.

* * *

There was enough left of the framework of Guido's to board up with big sheets of graffiti-encrusted plywood. It was silent down here, except for the sound of the occasional waves and distant traffic noises. The charred timbers stood out against the sky, in front of the shore, under the moon's soft glow. What was left of the awning, its tattered remnants blowing in the breeze, obscured the front door.

I thought I saw light coming from behind the plywood. It had to be an illusion, some reflection of the moonlight. Suddenly, two figures advanced from beneath the awning. A man and a woman, young. The man had a gun.

"Hands up, mister," he said.

A simple enough command. I complied. I didn't have more than forty dollars on me. I started thinking about identity theft, about what I'd need to do if they took all my ID with my wallet. Would they let me go, or beat the life out of me? And what if they found the gun?

Then I saw they were both vampires. I felt myself relax.

The female searched me and took my gun while the male vampire held his pistol on me and smiled a hard smile. She missed the knife on my leg holster, didn't get down that far. Amateurs.

The smirking male led me beneath the awning to the restaurant's door.

Inside, I found Bill.

He sat in a beat-up chair. He had a light bulb strung up in the charred rafters, a cable running back to a generator I could hear working outside.

"Sorry about the security," he said. Even with his thick beard,

Bill's face looked pinched. His long hair, tied in a ponytail, was greasy, as though he hadn't washed in a while. Worry lines ran from the corners of his eyes.

"I'm hiding out here," he said.

Bill always was one to state the obvious. He stood and I hugged him, a big bear hug.

He had a second chair arranged next to his, a card table between them piled with papers. Still working. I sat down in the chair.

"What about VARAS, Bill?" I asked.

I was in no mood to waste time. Bill sighed and nodded.

"It's the telomeres, Brand," he said.

Telomeres. So that was it. Telomeres are the part of our cells that control aging. They shorten a little every time a cell divides. When they get too short, they die. So do we.

"Vampire telomeres work differently than ours. It's what gives them their amazing longevity. A couple of Czech scientists were working on human life extension using Vampire telomeres. They developed a form of gene therapy that can extend the human life span up to thirty percent."

"Wow."

"Yeah," he said. He blinked, and signs of exhaustion worked their way out from beneath his steady expression. "But there's a catch. The same injection that will give you or me an increased life span will do just the opposite to a vampire. Inject Dracula with the gene soup, and he begins to die."

"So, we slap a warning label on it. Do not use if you're pregnant, nursing, or undead."

"It's not that simple." Bill rubbed his eyes. "There are people in this world that would be perfectly happy to perform a cellular genocide on our fanged friends. The fanatics, Human Firsters. They got hold of some of the stuff, after the Czechs synthesized it. Word is, there's an aerosol version out now, that's being sprayed wherever vampires are found. To disinfect the world of them."

"What can I do?" I asked.

He fished in his pocket, and handed me a test tube, full of a clear liquid.

"This is it," he said, "the stuff. If you analyze it, you might be able to develop an antidote."

I looked at the liquid in the tube. It seemed to sparkle in the weak light. I slid the test tube into my jacket pocket.

"I'm counting on you, Brandon," Bill said.

A moment later, there was a sound like thunder, and Bill's head exploded.

I yelled, a long crazy yell, and kicked the chair over. I felt my eyes dilate, felt myself going into shock. My heart pounded nearly out of my chest.

My training took over. I reached in my pocket for my gun. It was gone.

"Keep your hands where I can see them," Aesha said.

She moved toward me, her face blank and beautiful like a Barbie doll, her eyes narrowed. She held a vintage Colt .45 on my head. The gun looked bigger than she was.

I shot a glance behind her. The two young vampires were lying dead at the door, headless, garroted. With a silver garrote, no doubt, and silently -- the work of a professional. A dark crimson stain spread on the floor around them.

"Sit down," she commanded.

I pulled the chair up and complied.

"Thanks, Royce," she said, "Thanks for leading me right to him."

"Why'd you do it, Aesha?"

"I need to make a living," she said, grinning now, gliding toward me, "and I'm tired of the escort service racket."

My mind ran a thousand miles a minute.

"Who are you working for? The Czechs? The Human Firsters? The Firsters wouldn't like your kind much, Aesha."

Aesha wore a frilly little red number that barely covered her assets. She did a little flick with her left hand, and it slid off, leaving her naked like the night before. She stepped out of it, and moved lithely, with the pistol still in her right hand.

"I like you, Dr. Royce," she said, "I like you a lot. So I'm going to make a deal with you. Give me the formula Bill gave you, and you can have me. All night long, if you want."

"Heck of a deal," I said, "Your boyfriends end up in your belly, baby."

"You don't understand."

"Oh, I understand, all right. Mate, then feed."

"No, you don't," she said.

Then, to my astonishment, I saw a tear starting to trickle down her perfect, right cheek.

"You don't know anything! I loved them all, and they loved me, too! Every one of them!"

"Yeah, baby," I said, "They loved you, right through their dying screams."

A fire lit up behind her eyes.

"They never screamed!" Aesha cried, "You don't know anything about it! You don't know what it's like to be inside of me!"

Her trembling body impacted me at some far-off level, like a gorgeous babe in the kind of book you read one-handed.

"They all felt wonderful, happy. Full of joy for the first time in their lives! Even while I was feeding on them. Especially while I was feeding on them!"

"Sounds like my idea of post-coital bliss."

She shot a poisonous glance at me.

"You don't know anything! My body produces an anesthetic a thousand times more potent than any street drug. Street drugs work for a moment, dulling the pain of existence. But the man who climaxes inside of me feels a bliss that goes way beyond the moment! Beyond space, beyond time!"

She was circling me now as she spoke, her hips swinging. Space and time. Something about her made me think of every girl I'd ever known, from the innocent little kid I'd had a crush on in Junior High, to the first girl I'd ever laid, my senior year in high school, to all the girls I knew in college and med school. And to Julie, God help me, to Julie.

"I provide a bliss that does more than just insulate my lover from pain. My bliss works backwards, through the whole stained pages of his life, healing every bit of pain he ever felt, cleansing every dirty moment, every sorry memory, reworking all of it until he knows why he lived, his reason for being. To be absorbed in me, to feed me! And in the end, they feed me gladly!"

She stood there, after her soliloquy that echoed a little into the rafters, her gun still pointed at my forehead. I could tell she was proud of herself, of her eloquence. But I thought that if Hitler had been a woman, well, this was just how he would have talked.

I watched her belly rise and fall. She would eat a guy, or maybe two or three, then give birth to a child, without even losing her figure. A girl child, always a girl. A thing that never suckled, a thing with teeth that ate meat from day one.

Shakespeare got it wrong. Lady Macbeth should birth only girl children. Girl children, just like herself. It was a funny form of recycling. I forced a smile.

"Sounds wonderful," I said, "but Bill didn't give me the formula."

She didn't look disappointed. She was all business now.

"Where is it?" she asked.

"In a safety deposit box," I lied, "I have the key on me."

"Give me the key."

I hesitated, then bent over. I heard her cock the .45.

"Easy, baby," I said, raising my left hand, while I rolled up the pant leg with my right, "It's inside my right sock."

Later, I would wonder how I did it. I would even try to retrace my movements, to replicate it. But I couldn't. It was all subconscious, a feat of the moment, something I could only have done in the face of death. Something Aesha, confident in the power of her hypnotic sexuality, never anticipated.

With a single movement of my wrist, I extracted the silver scalpel from its holster, flipped it around between my thumb and forefinger, and scythed it a split-second later through the air at Aesha. It found its target perfectly, slicing through her thumb, taking the gun from her hand with it.

Disarmed, she screamed a blood-curdling scream. I popped to my feet, upended the table, and headed straight for her, intending to tackle her to the floor. When I collided with her, however, I found that she was the immovable object. She roared and grabbed me with her claw-like hands by the shoulder and twisted around, her steely animal musculature far stronger than I'd anticipated. Then she threw me against the wall.

I landed hard. On her hands and knees, Aesha scrambled for her gun.

I saw mine, the .38, lying next to one of the dead vampires. We both skittered forward and managed to re-arm ourselves, fumbling, at the same time.

Then Aesha made her fatal mistake. She took the time to come up to her knees and aim. I wasn't so dainty. I fired wildly, behind me.

I came up a winner. The slug hit her right between the breasts, knocking her over, dislodging her own weapon from her already-wounded hand.

I got to my feet and walked over to her. As I stood over her prone body I saw that she was still alive, struggling. There was very little blood yet, just a little hole in her chest. Her lungs made a sucking sound as she fought for breath.

"Finish me," she managed with a hideous gasp, her eyes wide and unfocused, blood foaming from her mouth.

I'm a doctor. It's my mission to heal, not to kill. Not to kill, even by request.

I thought about Aesha as I stared down at her. How much of a woman was she? How much was she a person that could love and hope and dream? And how much was she just a monster, a predatory beast pretending to be a warm-blooded member of our species?

And why should that even matter to me? I've made my life's work helping things like her, creatures, despised monsters, to live and to survive. I've always believed that even the most hideous creatures were worthy of life.

If I'd tried, I probably could have saved Aesha's life. Got her back to the clinic to perform emergency surgery. She'd have been scarred, no longer perfect, but she'd be alive.

Aesha looked at me, struggling to make her lips move again. I thought about how she'd killed my friend, Bill Hathaway. About how she'd tried to kill me.

"Goodbye, baby," I said.

I pointed the .38 between the Harridan's eyes, and pulled the trigger.

I shot out the light bulb, up in the rafters, and left the carnage behind me in the abandoned restaurant. I heard sirens in the distance as I walked away into the night.

I had an antidote to prepare. An antidote to VARAS that would save lives. The lives of vampires, creatures that would go on to feed on other lives once I cured them. The lives of humans, just like me.

But, then, vampires are my patients. I have a duty to save them. All of them, if I can.

And if that wasn't enough, there was Bill Hathaway's death. He died to save them all.

And if it was up to me, his death wasn't going to be in vain.

The End

About the author: *H. F. Gibbard is a lawyer by day and a writer of speculative fiction by night. His speculative fiction has appeared or is forthcoming in anthologies, online 'zines and print venues including Anotherealm, Aoife's Kiss, Astounding Tales, Cybertales: Live Wire, Fried: Fast Food, Slow Deaths, GateWay SF, Razar Magazine, Static Movement, Theatre of Decay, and Would That it Were. He also writes a legal history column for the Colorado Lawyer magazine*

Renegade Angel

Paranormal Mystery Storyline edited by Elysabeth Eldering

Little Girls

by Batya Deene

Dear Readers,

Renegade Angel - Dylan Holter - an ex-cop, turned private detective, dead and gone wild.

Welcome to the mystery section of Unbelievable Stories. This is where we meet the ghost of Dylan Holter who struggles to solve his cold cases.

When Dylan Holter's life is prematurely taken by a fire, he sets out for revenge. He revolts against the whole dying thing and makes his only purpose resolving the cases he left behind. If for nothing else, closure. The families deserved it. Every case file that burned up with Dylan must be solved. Dylan has to somehow come up with a way to communicate with someone to help him solve the cases.

As each mystery unfolds, we are taken on many rides, but all lead to the resolution of Dylan's old cases. I have searched for the unusual, very creative cases and hope you all enjoy the stories as much as I have.

Elysabeth Eldering
Mystery Editor

Little Girls

"Lord, it's bright here. Turn those lights down!" I squinted but couldn't see a friggin' thing. My eyes burned from that pervasive white light. My work's primarily done at night, or in dark alleys, or poorly lit offices. I'm perpetually behind shades so I can't be recognized, and because it's de rigueur costuming for a P.I.

"Who are you?" I yelled. "Get those things off me!" I shook my arms as two white-sheeted creatures grabbed me from behind. "Oh, geez, not wings! I'm not a wing-wearin' type of guy, can't you tell?" Was this some sort of Halloween joke? It took all my energy, but I shook them off. "Hey, where am I?"

It's about then I noticed the eerie sound of a stringed instrument, something between a guitar and violin. It irks me when I can't identify things exactly. I'm trained to notice the details. Any PI worth his salt would be out of business---or dead---pretty quick if he didn't.

Dead? Did I just say 'dead'?

"Hey, where am I?" I shouted into the infernal light. Nothing.

I tried my memory: Lots of gore and guts but nothing that might have brought me here. Wherever here was.

"I'm not kidding. Somebody tell me where I am. Right now!" I'm not used to being ignored, not unless I'm trying to be invisible. Some of those stakeouts required a lot of invisibility, and I'm not talking about a magic cloak, either. I'm talking the knack of disappearing into the scenery, melting into the milieu. Other than that I've always liked being the center of attention, especially if there's a pretty skirt around. But it wasn't a pretty skirt's voice that called my name.

"Dylan Holter." It was deep and sounded far away. I looked up, down, sideways...nothing. "Dylan Holter," it repeated.

"Yeah, that's me. Who are you? Where are you? Where am I?"

"Dylan Holter...you're at the gates of Heaven."

"Heaven? Me? I don't think so. I don't see gates. Besides, I'm not dead."

The voice continued. "Think, Dylan Holter. Think back to this morning. Where were you?"

I forced my brain back into the activity of memory, and it wasn't easy. "Home. Morning. Funny smell. Couldn't breathe." I paused.

"And?" the voice boomed.

"And....I tried to get the blankets off me...hot, too hot. Had a hard time breathing, moving. God, it hurt."

"I'm sorry about that, but some things in My creation still have their secrets. What do you remember next?"

"Um..." I tried harder. "There were flames. Fire—yeah, fire. Coughing. I tried to roll off the bed onto the floor. Everything was burning. My notes, my files. Electric cords like fiery snakes, furniture melted like lava across the floor, the curtains erupted like a furnace blast. The heat. The stench of flesh and hair burning. My flesh. My hair. Oh my God. You mean...really? I'm dead?"

"Exactly correct," the voice felt closer, warm, soothing. "Welcome to Heaven, Dylan Holter."

"No way."

"What do you mean 'no way'? Do you know who I am?"

"Well, I figure you're either God or the Angel of Death. Maybe Saint Peter. Am I close?"

"Right on your first guess."

"Look dude, God, whatever You are...I'm not ready to be dead. I'm forty-four years old; I just gave up all my fun times to get engaged. Me monogamous? Doesn't that deserve a reward, not death? I can't leave Kitty alone. It'll break her heart. That's just not right. Besides, that Michael O'whatever-his-name-is has just been waiting for an excuse to move in and steal her. Besides, what about all the people counting on me to find thieves, murderers, kidnappers, cheating husbands and wives, insurance frauds? I can't be dead. I'll have to recreate all that information that burned. I'm too busy to be dead."

"Busyness has nothing to do with it."

"Well...thanks for the invite into Heaven, but I'm heading back. Gonna find whoever set that fire, make sure he spends his life behind bars."

"Dylan Holter. You're not understanding. You're dead. You live here now."

"No way." I knew I was repeating myself, but couldn't find better words for it. "I'm going back. Hey, look at it this way for a minute."

"I'm listening."

"Thanks." I wasn't quite sure if after all this arguing I'd still be welcome in Heaven, but what the hell? I liked my life---at least since I quit the police force with all its rules and regulations that let the perps loose. I'll be damned if those scums didn't have more rights than I did. Going out on my own, making my own rules, my own hours, choosing the jobs I want and leaving the rest for others....perfect kind of life.

"You've got to send me back," I insisted. "That wasn't a chance fire, was it?" I took the silence for agreement. "I bet it was the punk who raped those little girls behind the churches. Police gave up on the search, but I've got my contacts and clues. You can't possibly like Your house of worship used that way. I almost had him. Don't You want justice?"

"But you didn't catch him. And you're dead now. And I'm the One who metes out justice, not you." The white around me shimmered, no, rippled. Like the voice had the power to move the light.

"I don't have to be dead. Right? It's a ridiculous rule You've got. Someone's dead and they have to stay dead. Who thought that one up? You? Well, every rule *should* be broken now and then. And now's the time to break it. Send me back. You won't be sorry."

"You can't go back. Your body's been buried."

That stopped me. I gazed down at myself, at least where myself used to be. Sure, I still had arms and legs and my tough-as-nails abs---I worked hard for those. But I was see-through. All the way through. That wasn't right. Transparent is less my style than wings. I took a deep breath.

"Well, then, let's get creative here," I argued. "There's gotta be a way for me to go back, finish what needs finishing, tie up loose ends, that sort of thing."

"You're very persistent, Dylan Holter."

"I've been called worse."

He laughed. He actually laughed. It wasn't even a new joke. He had to have heard it before.

"Look, God..." I was beginning to realize how

shaky the mist I stood on was, but I'm not one to give up till I get what I'm looking for. "Can't You just create me a new body?"

"No." He stopped laughing. "But let Me think here a minute."

"Sure, but don't take too long...no telling where the scum's getting to while I'm twiddling my thumbs up yonder here."

The silence seemed like an eternity. Maybe it was.

"Fine, here's the deal. You're going back, but you don't get another body. Take this one with you. I'm warning you---no one will see you, and no one will hear you."

"How the hell am I gonna catch this guy then?"

"Watch that, Dylan Holter. It's as far as I'm willing to work with you. You need to be thanking Me as I've granted your after-dying wish. Find someone back there to help you. That's the deal."

"I'll take it," I said, but I don't think He heard me. By the time I finished saying 'take' I felt a whooshing and fell butt first onto Broadway and 42nd Street, in the heart of the theater-and-whores district of Manhattan.

Cars rolled over me. They didn't feel the bump, and I didn't feel their weight. I've been in strange situations

before, but nothing like that. Shock? Oh, yeah. I could tell, right from the start, this wasn't going to be my easiest assignment. Looking back on it, I'm still surprised at what I didn't notice, all the things that had changed. Like the models of the cars rolling over and through me. Amazing what a new ghost misses while focusing on its ghostliness.

First things first. I figured I'd go back to my place, see if anything useful had survived the fire. What I expected to see wasn't there: charred wood beams, cracked and fallen roof tiles, an exposed porcelain tub and sink with gray streaks across them, maybe my file cabinet, the one I kept locked...was that too much to hope for?

Seems it was.

Where my apartment had stood, bracketed by other apartments in a building cushioned by other buildings, was an empty lot. Nothing. Not even the remains of a city mouse. Not a pigeon dropping. Not a brick. That was quick. Never saw New York clean up a mess that fast before.

Right there, on that empty lot that had the audacity to be vacant, I sat. How could I possibly solve anything when I couldn't be seen, felt, heard, or even mourned? I grabbed a pebble and threw it---at least that's what I thought I did. The pebble didn't move.

I was insubstantial.

Have you ever seen a depressed ghost? We're not pretty. The best we can manage is half a howl in the night, but only if there's a full moon and it's midnight, no clouds, and Wednesday---or Halloween. Well, I'm exaggerating about the Wednesday part, but the rest is true.

So I wandered. More alone than the loneliest person on Earth. Hey, I told you I was depressed...depressed ghosts throw pity parties, too. Finally I got myself up and about, determined to bring justice to the subhuman who hurt those little girls.

With all the stories about hauntings, and all the talk shows and magazine articles that always pop up about those who converse with the dead, I thought I'd be able to make contact with someone. Must have been three weeks that I floated around going 'Boo!' to every person I passed. Not one flinched. Not a sneeze. Not a hiccup.

Okay, I'm thinking, there's gotta be another way.

So I started haunting dreams. That's not easy. As a ghost, I had to put a lot of effort into it, without really knowing if I was getting any results. I mean, I couldn't float into their dreams to see.

Finally, I got one. A young woman who happened to live about three blocks from my old place. I spent the night whispering into her right ear. The chick's a hard sleeper, didn't turn over once. So there I am, telling her all the details I could remember about the guy who killed those girls and possibly burned my place down. I wasn't sure they were connected, but there was a good chance.

She scared me half to death—if I hadn't been dead already I think I'd have had a heart attack—the way she jumped wide awake from a deep sleep.

"Holy Jehosephat!" she said, clear as anything. "What was that about?" She slung her rather shapely legs over the side of the bed, shuffled around for slippers, stuck her toes deep into them, and headed for the bathroom in the cutest pink pajama short set I'd ever seen. I gave her some respect and stayed in the bedroom, but I could hear her muttering. "What a dream! Three girls dead and a fire. Where'd that come from?

I must be working too hard." And then she stopped talking to herself. Or the water in the shower drowned her out. But she'd gotten the dream, and I decided to follow her around, see what she might do with all that information. If she remembered any of it.

Being the gentleman I was---or maybe it was my short stint in Heaven---I waited in the hall for her to dress. When she appeared in jeans, a white T-shirt under a striped blue and white shirt, and sneakers, she reminded me of someone, but I couldn't put my finger on a name. This specter stuff sure did mess with my brain waves. She looked good, though: casual, put-together, determined. She closed the door before I could follow her out, but passing through it proved no problem at all.

In a few short blocks--- after a stop at a fancy coffee shop where she picked up a white chocolate latte, whatever the hell that is---we reached my old home-away-from home, the good ol' precinct. I wondered what we were doing there. The building looked the same from outside: old redbrick that desperately needed washing. Inside too, at first: the information desk with a uniform in charge, the poor lighting in the entry hall.

She flashed her ID for entrance; I didn't need one anymore.

A few steps inside, though, and I realized everything had changed. First, I didn't recognize anyone: None of the ol' boys puffin' on cigarettes, throwing curses around the room, pecking at electric typewriters; no dingy gray walls obscured by papers hanging every which way, with Help Wanted posters tacked on the pillars. Who chose rosy pink for the walls in here? And why didn't I smell fresh paint? I'd been there only a few days ago.

Everything was neat: Rows of photos in alphabetical order on bulletin boards, cases and investigators listed in neat handwriting on a blackboard, a computer on each desk---and computers like I'd never seen, that's for sure. Thin little screens, keyboards on rolling drawers; the hum of them all laid a backdrop for the clicking of keys and the few conversations that went on. There was more light, too; they'd replaced the little desk lamps with improved hanging fixtures. Even the floor had been re-laid: no more black and white checked linoleum squares. Instead, some sort of wood-looking flooring spread underfoot. And where did they find all these female cops? Things sure changed a lot mighty fast. And the Chief's office, which sat in the same location, was now encapsulated behind a glass wall. He could see out, but all the detectives could see in, too. That wasn't such a good idea in my day.

In my day. Yeah. That proved to be longer ago than I'd thought. I caught sight of a calendar on one of the desks: exactly twenty-five years to the day after I'd burned to death. Imagine that. Didn't think my conversation with the Lord had lasted quite that long, but it explained the new model cars and the computers. Nothing could explain the pink walls.

Maybe it took twenty-five years to change my luck. From the millions of possible embodied humans in Manhattan, I'd chosen one that could actually help nail the bastard who raped and killed those little girls: Detective Lanna O'Malley, the plate said on her desk. Now all I had to do was direct her to the case.

Turns out Lanna O'Malley was the rookie detective, and, therefore, had been delegated the Cold Case files. A few stacks of them sat along the front edge of her desk, and by peering over her shoulder as she turned on the computer and started flipping through her files there, I could see she was just getting started. My job would be to find a way to get her to the relevant file---and unless someone else had put it in the computer, she was looking in the wrong direction.

I remembered that Detective Longo had investigated. He'd called me when he'd hit the brick walls. No witnesses, no clues, no disruption of anything but the three little girls' lives. Three dead little bodies and one very gone perp.

"Marshall," he'd said when he finally called me in on it. That's what the guys baptized me soon's they heard I was dating Kitty: Marshall Dylan. Started as a joke, but it stuck. "I've got a bad feeling about this, but I've got all dead ends. See what you can do without the restraints, would you?"

I couldn't resist taking it on. For one thing, I was bored at the time. I mean, there's only so many stakeouts a guy can do looking for a cheating wife before he dies of boredom. Besides, catching child molesters was a favorite of mine. Of all the reprobates I brought down in my life, the only ones I roughed up when I had the chance were those who hurt kids. Who beat them. Or sold them drugs. Raped them. Those were the perps who couldn't stand up even before they got behind bars, least not if I was the one who helped put them there. Not all of them were men, either. And no one ever called me on it---not a cop, not a judge, not a journalist: at least not after I turned the badge in for private work. One of the many perks of being a renegade.

But I digress.

Here I was, back in the old haunting grounds, to re-coin the phrase, sure one of those mildew-smelling files contained the case of the three little girls, and no way of telling my new partner which one. Or even to look for that case. Big dilemma. So I huffed, and I puffed, and I pulled all my ghostly energy into one effort, and I bumped my incorporeal arm into the stack of folders and toppled them to the floor. Took so much effort I found myself fallen over, too. But there it was, spread out beside my left eye, top of the pile: Borger, Ellen; age 8; Simmons, Traci, age 6; Hellman, Sandra, age 9.

"Shit!" Detective Lanna shrieked as she spilled latte and jumped up to grab a stray paper. She missed, and it joined the others on the floor. When she ran around the desk and bent down to gather them all up, I rolled away from her hand. That was the first time ever I'd avoided a pretty woman's touch, and I wasn't quite sure why I did it then, but there was something about this chick that made physical distance imperative. Maybe it was the ghostness, maybe something else. Whatever, her attention focused on the papers about the girls, and when she straightened everything, including herself, up, she pulled the folder out and started reading.

The girls had nothing in common except that they went to church, though not the same church. They weren't friends, attended different schools, didn't play in the same parks; their parents didn't know each other beyond a passing nod of the head in the supermarket. Two were white, one black. Nothing to tie them together besides all of them being at the wrong place at the wrong time and dying too early by the same means: suffocation. The first was raped before she died, the other two after. Lanna read through every detail: interviews with church-goers, transcription of tapes with grieving family members, talks with the pastors, Longo's name, my name. And too much blank space where evidence and clues belonged.

She closed the file, leaned back in the creaky chair---that hadn't changed since my time---and closed her eyes. I imagined she was imagining the crimes, something we all did in our idiosyncratic ways. There was a tear, though, that escaped from the outside corner of her left eye and took its damn time before dropping. She shook herself, ran her fingers through her curled brown hair and sat straight up. I could tell she was going to pass on the case, and I couldn't have that.

So I stood right over her; she was inside me, like a lunch sandwich inside plastic wrap, occupying the same space. Although I had no voice, I kept repeating, 'This is the one, you can do it. This is the one.' Over and over until she flipped the cover back again and stared at the pictures taped to the inside cover.

"Okay," she said. "Where do I start?" I had an idea, but telling her would be the hard part. It surprised me, how exhausted a ghost could get. I needed a break. My mouth watered for a half-stale donut and a really bad

cup of coffee. That familiar smell came from the same corner; the coffeemaker, in a newer model, perked away just like it always had. Strange, the things that made me most regret dying.

Turns out she didn't need me to get started, after all. Good instinct, this one.

These new computers are wonders. She banged some letters on the keyboard, clicked the mouse a few times, and a screen popped up with information about child rape-and-murder cases across the country from a few years before the three girls until present. With a bit more refinement, Lanna trimmed the list down. It was still too long---one name would have been too long the way I see it---but now it was manageable. 'That's my girl!' I ghost-whispered at her.

She turned. I could have sworn she was about to answer me, but she only blinked, then refocused on the screen. She had honed the list a few times. First, raped girls, cutting out the boys. Then she typed in an age parameter: four to twelve, a little wide of the victims, but I'd have done the same. Her list was limited to the five boroughs; after a quick look through it, she widened it to the Northeastern

United States. That added too many screens.

'Type in churches,' I suggested. She flicked her hand across her ear, like a fly had buzzed there. Progress, I thought to myself. Either my ghost voice had strengthened, or she was tuning to me. Or there was just some dumb luck at work here. She typed in *churches*, and waited as the computer droned. Here was information even I hadn't had. Twenty-six similar crimes; the only difference being that the later ones sometimes involved a knife across the neck instead of suffocation. Twenty six dead little girls over a three-year period. And none of the murders had been solved. Of course, the states of New York, New Jersey, Connecticut, Vermont, New Hampshire, Maine, and Massachusetts didn't always confer, but you'd think the FBI would have gotten wind of some of this.

This perp was the Devil himself.

Lanna whistled. Then she took a bottle of Excedrin from her drawer and swallowed one with the now-tepid latte. Yup, gonna be long day. I hadn't gotten this far, not in this direction. I'd assumed the perp was local, staying local. But after my three, there weren't any

similar deaths in the area for years. He'd moved on.

She called up and read every file that had been scanned into the database, and I read over her shoulder. No one had evidence. And the two ripped pages I'd found had burned into ash more than two decades ago.

Opening a clean screen, Lanna typed her notes.

```
• Every one of these
  little girls died near
  a church, or were
  transported to the
  location

• Every one raped; before
  death or after. Looks
  like the same scumbag
  moved to New York from
  Jersey, then headed
  northeast, through
  Connecticut and onward.

• Between 2 and 5 in any
  one place.

• No ritual details
  evident; odd, given the
  locale.

• Search church records,
  check real estate
  sales, anyone from here
  move to CT?

• Track any priests,
  reverends, etc., choir
  members, cleaning
  staff.

• What day of the
  week….
```

Lanna stopped typing, flipped to the previous screen, scanned down the list, pulled up a calendar. I was amazed at what the girl could do with a computer. "Damn," she muttered. "Every single one on a Sunday." She flipped back to her notes.

- **Check Sunday School teachers and helpers.**

- **Hartford records...next place he went.**

- **Go to the churches.**

That's my girl, I thought again. Thorough. I got ready to leave. But she wasn't jumping up so fast. First, she made a call. Four digits: internal.

"Brad, hey, it's Lanna," she said into the receiver.

I leaned my ghost-ear close enough to hear the whole conversation.

"Honey, how are you? Are we on for tonight? Six o'clock? La Vin, usual table?"

"Sure," Lanna blushed, smiled. "But I need your help."

"Anything for you, sweetheart. Name it."

Something inside me clicked into pure hatred for this guy, and I couldn't figure out why.

"I need you to run some searches for me. Brad, I know you have more important things keeping you busy in the dungeon, but if you have an extra minute here and there..."

"This on a cold one, Lanna?"

"Yeah."

"Not about your father again, is it?"

"No, not directly."

"You gotta give up on that, honey."

Lanna sighed, leaned her forehead in her free palm. "It's not about him. It's about twenty-some-odd dead little girls."

"Give it to me, baby."

She described what she needed, confirmed six o'clock for dinner, thanked Brad, and hung up. Smiling, she gathered her badge and her bag, and headed out. I followed at her heels.

Our first stop was The Little Church of the Holy Name, tucked between two rows of brownstones on West 17th Street. The iron gate welcomed guests with open arms, and we walked straight through the front garden with its manicured lawn and curve of shrubbery to the door. A buzzer stopped us, but not for long. Lanna flashed her identity card at the surveillance camera---what's this world coming to, churches needing high-tech security?---and they rang us in. Well, they rang her in: I scooted in on a free ride. A white-haired woman in a tidy yellow suit emerged from a doorway, indicated that Lanna follow her into the office.

"Thank you," Lanna said. "I'm here to see the pastor, if I may."

"Pastor Merrifield or Pastor Lanoy?"

"Which one was here twenty-five years ago?" Lanna asked.

"That would be Pastor Merrifield. He's in, I believe." She used a phone as outdated as herself, dialed a few numbers, mumbled into the receiver. She hung up quickly. "Follow me, please." We did just that.

The pastor waited by a stained glass window, its diamonds separated by gray steel that matched the color of his hair. He stood looking out for another moment, though how he could see through the colored panels I didn't know. Even slightly stooped with his shoulders rounded forward, the man's stature was impressive. I wouldn't have wanted to meet him down a dark alley, even with our age difference.

"Please have a seat." Lanna sat. I remained close

by, at her left elbow. "Coffee?" Lanna indicated No, thanks, with her head. "How can I help you?"

"I'm investigating the rape and death of Traci Simmons."

"Oh my, my. That was some time ago." The pastor took his chair, leaned forward.

"Anything you remember about that time that was odd? Anything you might have thought about since then?"

"Give me a minute here. Memory takes a while at my age. I believe I gave the investigating officers all the information I had at the time. Maybe if you ask me specifics that'll jog the old brain a bit."

"You were the pastor then?"

"Junior pastor. I'd been assigned this flock two years earlier, my third assignment since the seminary, I believe. Pastor Jenkins had the senior position. He passed on a few years ago."

"Was there anyone in your congregation you felt uncomfortable with? Any strangers? Anyone new to town who moved here from New Jersey, say?"

"New Jersey?" The pastor carefully placed his elbows on the desk, steepled his hands in front of him. "They say long-term memory improves about now, but I'm not remembering anything like that. We were a pretty settled community at the time, not a lot of folks moving in or out. A few of our parishioners moved uptown, or downtown, but they usually changed churches, too. At the time of little Traci's tragic death...no, I don't recall any new faces. The whole community was so upset, we held a number of additional prayers; people came together to console her family. No one out of the ordinary. I would have noticed, I'm sure."

"Did anyone join your church from Divine Light Baptist? Or leave to attend St. Cecelia's?"

He brought the steeple closer to his face, rested his chin in it. "Weren't those the churches where the other girls died?"

"Yes."

"An awful few years that was. People became too frightened to bring their children to church. Imagine that. But no, we're all different denominations, some might say different religions, but I believe that's a bit extreme. I don't remember any of our members being from or going to either of those churches."

"I understand they found Traci's body out back?"

"Yes, do you want to see the location?" Pastor Merrifield pushed his chair back.

"Please."

He took us out a rear door of the church into a garden. To the right stood a garage, freshly painted a dark green that blended in with its natural surroundings. To the left stood an old, rotting tool shed, close to toppling over. I recognized it immediately. He took us to it.

"May I look around?" Lanna asked.

"Of course," the pastor answered. "Just come back through the doors when you're done."

I knew Lanna wouldn't find a thing, since I'd been over the place two or three times back when, so I pretended to lean against one of the walls and enjoyed watching her work. She sure was thorough, in spite of how much old junk cluttered the small space. In the back corner, pulling aside a pile of discarded clothes, she found a final flutter of yellow tape. That got her going, and there wasn't a single cobweb or anthill left by the time she was done.

Turning toward the door, I thought she was ready to leave, but she turned back, bent down, found a ripped sheet of paper, faded to gray, with black print, some of it circled with a marker, maybe part of a page from a book; I couldn't see it clearly from where I stood, and before I got closer, she'd folded it and stuffed it into a plastic bag, which she then stuffed in her pocket. Dang, I thought, but less politely. I sure did want to know what that paper was about, especially if it was something I'd missed on my search of the premises. And if it matched in any way the pages I'd found. If so, it was the exact evidence that would nail the perp and fry his ass for whatever lifetime he had left. To say nothing of my going back to the Wild Blue Yonder and having another chat with God, mostly to get the perp's ass fried, well, for eternity.

After the thank-yous, and come-back-anytimes, and the sorry-I-couldn't-be-more-helps, we left. Lanna sat in the car for a minute, thinking to herself. I wish ghostness came with psychic powers, but it doesn't. She made a few calls, wrote some notes that I got to read. The Church of St. Cecelia had burned down about six years ago, the congregation splitting to neighboring churches instead of rebuilding. There were some names Lanna put on a

list, but I wasn't convinced she'd pursue it right off.

The Divine Light Baptist was out on Staten Island, so we headed for the ferry. Lanna flashed her ID and parked in the official area; seems cars aren't allowed on the ferry anymore. We just made last call for the 2:30. Lanna stood at the rail on the starboard side, facing the water; I preferred to watch Lower Manhattan recede. Once we hit the island, Lanna's classmate from the Academy, now assigned to the local force, met us; it was quite a drive out to the church, longer than I remembered, and they talked about things I either knew nothing about, or things I wanted to know nothing about: I had no idea why hearing about the whole Lanna-and-Brad thing got under my skin the way it did.

Even after all these years, the neighborhood where the Divine Light Baptist Church stood was remote, and it matched my memory exactly, even to the stand of three dogwood trees around a cement birdbath. Lanna strode through the church entrance as if she owned the place; I followed behind carefully, looking this way and that, focusing on anything I might have missed on my original go-through. Once she had permission, we wandered the grounds out back.

There used to be a shed, I thought, aiming it at Lanna.

"Was there ever a building or garage back here?" she asked the groundskeeper who'd followed us outside. Maybe this was getting easier for me; maybe we were both good detectives.

"Torn down years ago. We had a tragedy. Little girl died. Congregation voted on it and thought it fitting to turn the tool shed into kindling. Had a nice little bonfire. I was a teen back then, still remember the flames shooting straight up to Heaven when they shoulda been heading to Hell."

Poetry. What a thrill, I thought. Yup, ghosts can be cynical, too. I went and stood over the spot I remembered, still stained with young blood when I was called in. Like the grass and the earth refused to forget.

Lanna looked in my direction. "Over there?" she asked. The young man brought her right to me.

The area was overgrown now, a weed garden of sorts, sitting to the side of perfectly tended flower plots and carefully pruned shrubs. She shuffled through it, bending down to examine the ground, part the growth.

"What's this?" she asked, pulling a scrap of paper out from under a rock. The edges were tattered, the print barely legible. Leaning over her shoulder for a better look, I found the young man looking over her other shoulder.

"Looks like a hymnal," he said. "But we haven't used that one in years."

Lanna slipped it into another plastic bag before adding it to the contents of her pocket. "Any ideas?" she asked the groundskeeper. "Remember anyone moving in or out of the community back when the girl was killed? Anything you thought was off at all? Sometimes kids notice things that pass right by adults."

"Nah. We've always been a small community, even more rural back then. More folks leaving than coming in. Probably the last community with a Fuller brush salesman." He chuckled. "Had an old-man preacher, liked to lay on the fire and brimstone in his sermons, then lay back and swallow some fire and brimstone, if you know what I mean. He retired the year after Ellen's death. Drank himself to his own grave not long after. We're not a drinking community. But it wasn't him with the little girl.

Found out a few years later the old man preferred little boys to little girls. Had quite another scandal, almost destroyed the church. But, no, no strangers around."

"Thanks," Lanna said, passing him her card. "If you remember anything else..."

"Sure," he cut her off. "I'll call."

On the way back, I waited until the ferry ride before trying to reach her again. I knew she'd check for fingerprints on the scrap of paper, though after all these years, I didn't hold out much hope for useful results. 'Fuller brush man,' I shouted in my silent ghost voice.

She sat on one of the benches, staring out at the water, then grabbed her pencil and pad and started making yet another list. I peeked. Casper the curious ghost, that's me. *Fuller brush man* was right there at the top, followed by a question: *Passing-through?*

She had it! All that footwork and research and questioning parishioners that I'd gone through to reach the same conclusion...and here she just about had it in less than a day. I felt a strange pride in that.

Back at the precinct, she went straight to her buddy Brad. He sat in a windowless office surrounded by computers, rank mugs of coffee in various stages of abandonment, and an oversize Mr. Coffee perking away. Guess you had to be wired to connect with a computer the way he did.

"Get anything?" Lanna asked through a hug that lasted much too long.

"If nothing is anything, yup."

"I guess ruling things out is as important as ruling them in. Narrows the search." Lanna, obviously an optimist, said. That's okay, I thought, she's still young---and relatively new to the force. Disappointment, if not bad coffee, would erode that cheery attitude soon enough. She took the bagged papers from her pocket, used Brad's phone to call Evidence. People seemed to like her, and a girl appeared minutes later to gather the bags. "Soon as possible, Annie?" Lanna used her sweetest voice.

"Sure, I'll do my best. Child molesters never grow out of it...he could still be hurting little girls."

"Thanks," Lanna said to Annie's retreating back.

She returned to her desk, stopping for some of that bad coffee; bet there was ghost-drool on my lips. Again, she typed her thoughts---

which seemed to be her way of thinking things through: "Fuller brush man? Sales man? Church-goers knew him enough he wasn't noticed. A salesman would have a territory, region. Could it change every few years? Fuller brush...maybe. Who else? Vacuums? Milkman? Encyclopedias? Those were door-to-door back then."

I held my ghost-breath, afraid to interrupt her train of thought. It was almost exactly the same train I'd chugged along.

Lanna kept typing: "Church with encyclopedias, probably not. Other books? Bibles. Prayer books."

"Holy shit!" She didn't type that, but shouted it. No one in the room even looked up. BIBLE SALESMAN, she typed in all caps, then called the evidence room.

"I've got it," Annie said.

"Tell me, it's from a Bible? Or a prayer book? Hymnal?" Lanna got all that out in one breath.

"Yup, both of them. Same words circled...well, one was cut off, but the reference is there. They're not the same, but close."

"What are they?"

Annie paused before answering. "I looked it up and finished the quote: One is Matthew, 8:12, 'But the children of the kingdom shall be cast out into utter darkness: there shall be weeping and gnashing of teeth.' The second is Colossians 3:6, '...the wrath of God cometh on the children of disobedience.' "

"Thanks. I owe you one," Lanna said before hanging up. She dialed Brad again. "Brad, can you check evidence on these other murders? See if there were any Bible or prayer book pages found?...Thanks...yeah, ASAP."

It took a lot less time than I thought it would. Brad didn't call, but showed up, planted a kiss on Lanna's head before I could gather the ghost energy to Boo! him away from her. "Nothing in Connecticut. Perp got sloppy in New Hampshire and Maine, though." He typed something onto her computer and the screen that appeared had pictures of the evidence. I could make out the words clearly on one: Matthew 27:25, 'His blood be on us, and on our children.' What used to be my stomach wanted to heave.

That's it!! I shouted, though no one heard.

Lanna called Pastor Merrifield. "Did you have a traveling Bible salesman twenty-five years ago?" She paused for his answer. "Do you remember his name?" She grabbed a pen, wrote it down. "Thank you, you've been a great help." The smile spread across her whole face. "Got him! If you can find where he's located now, you can come along," she bribed Brad.

"Give me ten." He took over her computer, came up with an address out in Brooklyn within half that time. "Give me five more, I'll get my gear, meet you outside."

Hey, you don't need him, you've got me, I protested, to no avail at all.

We sped across the Brooklyn Bridge, wound our way through traffic on the Belt Parkway, exited in Bensonhurst, turned a few corners and stopped in front of Sam Peterson's Christian Book Store. Brad and Lanna jumped out, slamming the doors so I had to pass through the window.

"Sam Peterson?" Lanna asked the too-young clerk at the front counter.

"In back, but he's busy, doesn't want to be disturbed."

"We won't take long," Brad said.

All of us noticed that the children's book section was in the back corner of the store. There was a door there; Lanna turned the handle but it was locked from the other side.

"Open up, police!" Lanna called, her hand on her gun. My hand went to my holster, also, but I didn't have one. Brad, who must lift computers for strength training, kicked the door in; we heard some shuffling, turned to a room on the right.

A gray-haired, balding man in a plaid shirt, naked from the waist down, leaned over a wriggling child, his hand clasped across the girl's mouth and a knife at her throat. He had the smile of a maniac pasted across the lower half of his face, the upper half broken by eyes that stared at us with an unblinking coldness.

"Sam Peterson?" Lanna asked, following age-old procedure.

"That's me," he said, voice too calm for the situation.

"Let her go," Lanna said, her gun aimed at his heart with a steady hand.

"It's God's will," he replied with a demonic laugh. "One slice, she's dead." He moved the knife onto the girl's skin and a thin line of blood appeared. The girl turned pale, froze in place.

That was enough for me. I lunged. You've seen pictures of it, sheetlike ghosts floating through the air, graceful as the wind. Not like that. It took a lot of energy and I bounced a time or two, but there was so much fury in me that I actually think he felt it. I hit him full force, knocked the knife to the floor, pulled his hand from the child's mouth all at the same time. Brad jumped into the fray, tackled the guy down, cuffed him. Lanna held the little girl, talked to her in a soothing voice, called for support at the same time.

Guess we made a good team.

By the time Lanna got back to her desk to type up the report, I was feeling a little faded. Finding the guy who burned me and my place didn't feel quite as important anymore. There was a strange sense I had, like a pull, straight from the center of my belly, like a string, tightening, drawing me away.

I leaned over to plant a kiss on Lanna's lips as my goodbye, but she'd just leaned over to open her desk drawer and I got her forehead instead. "I finished it for you, Daddy," she whispered at the photo that lay there.

I recognized the picture. It was old, twenty-five years old, and I'd given it to Kitty about a week before the fire.

"Good job, Detective Dylanna Katherine O'Malley nee Holter," Brad said, gently placing his hands on her shoulders and his kiss on her hair. "Your Dad would have been proud of you."

Neither ghosts nor real men cry, and I was both, but tears fell straight from my ghost-heart. I love you, I said, as I floated toward the Light.

I'm certain I saw her look up.

The End

About the author: Batya Deene has been writing since age eight, and has published on and off since age nine. Publications include poetry, essays, nonfiction, travel, and CD liner notes. Presently, in addition to practicing psychotherapy in Nashville, Tennessee, she is working on a series of murder mysteries, writing Country music songs, and raising roses.

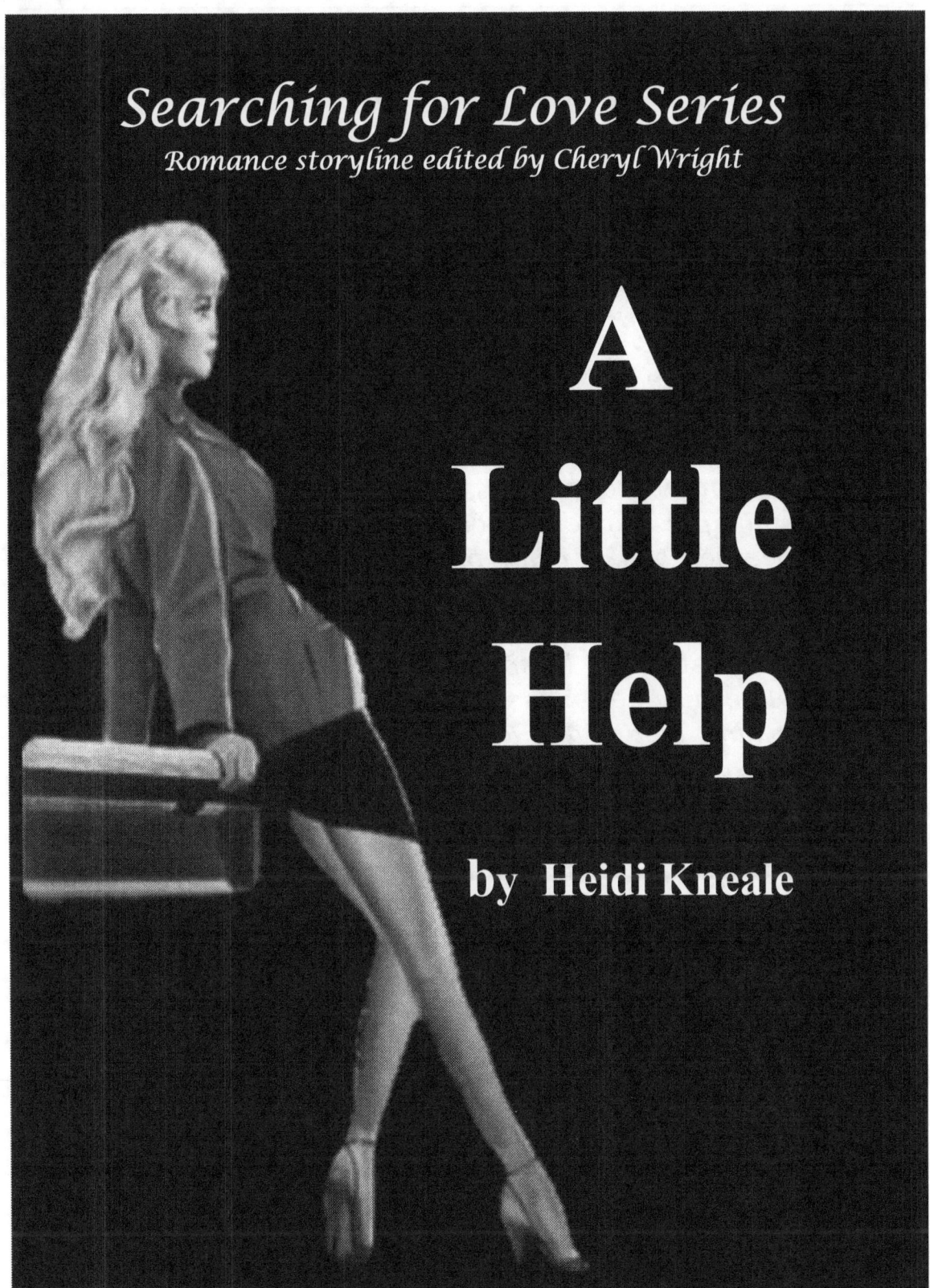

Searching for Love Series
Romance storyline edited by Cheryl Wright

A Little Help

by Heidi Kneale

Dear Readers,

Welcome to the romance storyline of The Magazine of Unbelievable Stories.

I wanted to give you something totally different with this series, so decided to shy away from what is generally accepted for romance. The writers were challenged to present stories out of the norm, and were given a lot of creative freedom.

What you will find presented over the next several months are the crème de la crème.

Each story has been hand-picked for originality and standard of writing, and has gone through a rigorous process before being accepted for publication. I hope you get as much pleasure from reading them, as I did from choosing each story, which centres around one main character: Sassy Brixton.

Sassy is an IT specialist and is very lonely. In her late twenties, Sassy realises that her body clock is ticking away, and despite her best efforts she's been unable to find the elusive "Mr. Right".

Instead of giving up on love, Sassy decides to aggressively pursue it, even to the extent of putting her best foot forward and taking control. If she's attracted, then she literally goes for it!

Each writer has brought an element to Sassy that other writers have not. You'll find her in various locations, and even in different worlds.

I hope you enjoy each story in this series, and look forward to your feedback.

Cheryl Wright,
Romance Editor

© Heidi Kneale

A Little Help

"Help Desk, this is Sassy." Sassy Brixton is used to having people come to her for help with their computer problems. But when she has love problems, she needs a little help herself. When a friend suggests a love spell to help catch the eye of the sexy Adel from Europe, Sassy gives it a try. If only she'd cast the spell correctly...

The Helpdesk phone rang. Sassy Brixton looked over at her co-worker and fellow Helpdesk prisoner, Dana Johnson. Dana pointed firmly at Sassy. "It's your turn."

Sassy groaned. She hated it when Dana was right. Securing her earphone and Alt-Tabbing out of her web browser into the call-logger, Sassy answered the phone. "Helpdesk, this is Sassy."

Hello, Sassy," said a sexy male voice that turned her stomach into jelly. "It's Adel again."

"Oh," replied Sassy. Her heart quickened and she wiped the sweat off her palms. Even though she'd known him for months, she had to fight the urge to squeal like a teenager whenever he called. "Hello, Adel."

Dana sat up, leaned over her desk towards Sassy and made googly eyes and kissy noises. Annoyed at her sudden embarrassment, Sassy waved her hand at Dana for her to go away. "What's the problem, Adel?"

Dana's phone rang and that got rid of Sassy's audience.

"I can't seem to connect to the department's printer." Adel's voice was a beautiful tenor lightly dusted with a continental European accent, maybe French, or perhaps Dutch. He belonged to some overseas branch of the company and had been transferred over for six months on a project. Sassy didn't know what, for every time she stopped by his desk to fix this problem or that, when she was done, she'd get awkward and tongue-tied and didn't know how to broach any subject beyond the computer.

"Okay," Sassy replied, her fingers tapping quickly on

the keyboard to log the call. "Are you connecting to any printers?"

"Um..." a moment of silence. "It tells me I'm connected to the double-slash Batavia slash lib forty-five hundred."

"Wow."

"What?" Dana said aloud. She'd just finished her phone call and turned her attention to something far more interesting? "He ask you out?"

No, Sassy mouthed at her. To Adel, she explained. "You shouldn't be connecting to the forty-five hundred at all. That's three floors down, and I'm sure you probably don't want to hike down three floors just to pick up your print job - unless you're fit. Uh..."

Dana had leaned across her desk again, pointedly listening to the conversation and batting her eyelids. Sassy turned away. "Hang on, I'll pull up the server and have a quick look at your profile. The batch file should be calling up the four-thousand printer. Just a moment."

As Sassy connected to the server, she felt the awkwardness of the silence between them. "So, Adel," she asked while she waited for the server to respond. "Where you from?"

"A little town called Nordwijkerhout."

She pulled up his profile and had a look at its properties. "Nerd-vicar-hoot, huh? That's, like, in Europe, right?"

Sassy realized how stupid she sounded as Dana planted her finger and thumb on her forehead in a letter L.

"Sorry," she apologized to Adel. "I'm distracted." She quickly changed the subject. "Your profile seems to be in order." She asked him a few more questions, such as did he log in three floors down (no), did someone from there log in his computer here (no), did he handle himself manually (what?)...

Dana burst out laughing. Sassy's face burned hot. "I mean, did you attempt to connect to the printer manually - you know, use 'Add Printer'?" Sassy put her hand over her microphone and mouthed a bad F-word.

"Can I do that?"

For a moment, Sassy thought she'd said the F-word out loud. "I'm sorry... If you want to... I mean..." Sassy didn't know what she meant.

Well, yes she did. She meant to saunter by his desk in slinky gown, fling her leg over his and settle into his lap to snog him until she sucked out his fillings. Then he'd whisk her away to Nerd-vicar-hoot where they could have a lovely little cottage somewhere and raise goats and tulips and little Adels.

She took a deep breath. "That is, it'll do you for now, but when you log out and log back in, you'll have to set it up again.

"Look," she said. "I don't know why your profile's giving you the wrong printer. I'll pop down and have a look."

Dana didn't wait for Sassy to hang up before commenting. "Yeah, I'm sure you'll have plenty to look at."

Sassy sighed. "Yeah. I could look at that face for the rest of my life. And when I wasn't looking at his face, I'd have his voice in my ear."

"You'd have other parts of him in other parts of you."

She grinned. "That too." Her countenance fell. "I think I love him, Dana."

Dana rolled her eyes. "Well, duh."

"I only wish he loved me too."

* * *

Adel had his own cubicle in a part of the office with a window. Sassy found the panorama of the city the second most spectacular view in that cubicle. Adel was tall and slim, with long blond hair he wore in a ponytail. Strands of it slipped forward around his face and he'd push them back behind his ears. His shoes were expensive (he was rich), his hands were bare of rings (he was single), and his eyes crinkled when he smiled at her (he liked her). And she really hoped all of that was true. She'd feel a right fool otherwise.

"Hi," she said, not leaning against his cubicle wall in case it fell over again. "Let's have a look at your computer." She leaned over him to take control of the mouse, her hand on the back of his chair for balance. Why didn't she wear a button-up shirt today so she could have undone a button before arriving?

Her skilled fingers dragged that mouse all over the computer, through the control panel and menus. "Huh," she uttered, momentarily forgetting the gorgeous man mere inches from her as she sorted through settings. "I have no idea why you're connected to the wrong printers. Let's log you out and log you back in so I can watch the batch file execute."

No answer. She looked at him. He sat there, his breath warm on her shoulder, staring up at her. Oh no. She didn't lose him, did she?

"That means," she explained, "that you'll have to save your work."

He stared at her for a moment longer. "Oh, okay." He brushed a stray lock of hair back behind his ear. "I'm afraid I don't know much about computers, but ask me the finer points of corporate contracts, and I'm your man."

Oh, I wish you were my man, Sassy thought.

Then a nasty thought occurred to her. What if he belonged to someone else. He might not be married, but what if he had a girlfriend back in Nerd-vicar-hoot, a serious girlfriend? Europeans were like that.

She took a risk and started a conversation while the computer rebooted. "So," she said, failing to not sound nervous, "what does your wife think of you traveling over here for six months?"

"I'm not married."

Oh, yes! "Oh, I'm sorry. I meant your girlfriend?"

"No, no girlfriend."

Oh, no. "Boyfriend?" Sassy squeaked.

Adel shook his head. "I'm quite unattached. That happens in a job like mine. No time to fall in love."

"Never?"

He smiled apologetically.

Sassy's heart broke. "So," she joked half-heartedly. "I guess drinks are out?"

He swiveled in his chair to face her straight on. Sassy squirmed, as her chest was level with his eyes. But it wasn't the girls he stared at, but up at her face. "Why do you ask?"

"Oh, look," Sassy blurted, "your computer's booted. Try logging in now."

As he logged in, she backed up, feeling as mawkish as she did when she was fifteen. The login fixed the problem and Adel's computer found the proper printers for his area.

"Thanks," he said with one of his crinkly smiles.

"Sure," she said as she leaned back against the wall of the cubicle.

Shame she forgot how unstable it was.

* * *

"I am fifty-seven kinds of fool!" Sassy ranted to Dana as soon as her co-worker was off her latest call. She spilled the details of her failed attempts to look sexy, her awkward questions about his personal life, followed by her total embarrassment of falling squarely on her posterior. "I don't know what hurts more, my bottom, my pride or my heart." She slumped at her desk and plunked her chin in her hands. "He's not interested in love."

"Poor Sassy," Dana crooned. "Your bottom's not as bad as you think because you've got enough padding to cushion your fall, your ego's bruised but not broken, and as for the last thing..." She smiled mysteriously, "I think I can help you with that."

Sassy glanced over at her friend. "Oh? You gonna kidnap him for me and leave him in my bedroom without any clothes?"

Dana shook her head. "I was thinking of a love spell."

Sassy snorted.

Dana held up a hand. "No, hear me out. They really do work. A cousin of mine used one to snag a guy. They're getting married next year."

Sassy sucked in air between her teeth. "I dunno, Dana. I never really believed in that sort of thing."

"C'mon," she cajoled. "It can only help, and nobody need know. You're not getting any younger."

In the back of her head Sassy heard the tick-tick of the clock that had kept her company since the day before her thirtieth birthday when she woke up and realized just how single she was. Two months later she had found a silver strand in her hair, and after two weeks' holiday in Acapulco, she had discovered the edges of her eyes had gone crepey. It was another year and a half until she had broken down and bought an eye cream. Then a lip cream. Then a rejuvenator. Then one day she looked in the mirror and wondered who this grown-up woman staring back at her was. She looked older than... well, older than she ought to be.

And really, was it fair she'd developed stretch marks? If she was going to have them, couldn't she have had a baby to go with it?

At least her breasts were okay, as long as she kept them in the bra.

"All right," she declared. "I'll do it, as long as it doesn't involve dancing naked in the moonlight."

* * *

Dana had sent her home with a shopping list for ordinary items. Later that evening, Sassy assembled her purchases with a few already-owned items on the kitchen table and examined them thoroughly. Yes, the cucumber was rather phallic, but Sassy guessed that was the point. The green paper wasn't too difficult to find and Sassy already had a few golden strands of Adel's hair, which she'd plucked from the back of his chair on one of her visits.

Bluetooth earpiece wedged into her ear, Sassy asked Dana over the phone, "Now what?"

"Take your cucumber and cover it in butter, using your fingers."

Sassy lifted the lid on the margarine tub and scooped out two fingersful. She greased the cucumber down, trying not to think sexual thoughts. "Okay, done." She wiped her fingers on a kitchen towel. "Now what?"

"Wrap the cucumber in the green paper, leaving both ends of the cucumber sticking out."

Sassy complied. "Okay. It looks like a green hot dog."

"Now take the rope you made from his hair and yours and tie the paper on."

It had taken Sassy twenty minutes earlier that evening before the slippery hairs obeyed her fingers and formed a tiny braided rope, and only once she figured she had to anchor the end to her pants with a safety pin. In the end, she had a rope long enough to tie around a cucumber. "Done."

Dana coughed. "Now, sprinkle some salt under your bed, lay a clean piece of white paper over the salt and lay the cucumber on that. As you go to sleep tonight, think about what you want the spell to accomplish. Keep that thought in your head. Then call me tomorrow morning as soon as you wake up."

Sassy nearly dropped the cucumber. "What? There's more?"

"Yeah. Tomorrow morning you've gotta slice up the cucumber and feed some of it to him."

Sassy let out a squeak of despair. "How on earth am I going to accomplish that?"

Dana groaned. "Look. If you really want this, you will find a way. True love always does."

A little thought nagged at Sassy's heart. "Dana?"

"Hmm?"

"What if this isn't true love?"

"Well," Dana replied, matter-of-factly, then you'll know it wasn't meant to be, and you can let go."

Sassy let her chin sink into her palm. "I don't want to let it go," she murmured, more to herself. She looked around her sparse apartment kitchen, with it's ugly clock on the wall, it's ancient microwave that begged for a good cleaning and the freezer full of microwave meals, single-serve. A lonely plate and cup sat in the drainer and a single pillow seemed too small for her double-bed in the bedroom. The other bedroom of her apartment didn't hold a little bed for a little sleeper with toys scattered across the floor, but a rather cluttered office with a hard, unhuggable computer. Sure, it was her 'baby', one she custom-built for her tastes and usage, but it wasn't the same.

A computer never hugged you back nor said, "I love you, Mommy."

"Sassy? Hello?"

Sassy shook the lonely thoughts out of her head. "Okay, does it matter what kind of salt?"

"No. Just get your salt-shaker and give it a few shakes under the bed."

Sassy complied. In the bedroom she scooted some dusty old books out from under the bed and sprinkled the salt. She laid the paper down and put the cucumber under there. "Sleep tight, little cucumber."

Sassy brushed her teeth and climbed into bed. The streetlight that shined through a crack in her curtains was just enough to show how empty the other side of her bed was. She laid a hand on the empty spot. "Not for long," she thought.

As she drifted off, she thought of Adel, with his fine blond hair, his voice touched by an accent and his smile that crinkled the edges of his eyes. She ran through her head what she was going to say to him tomorrow, something to entice him to try a slice of cucumber. Whatever you do," she admonished herself, "don't say something stupid."

* * *

The next morning in the office, Dana waited for Sassy. "So, do you have it?" The light on her phone blinked red; someone was on hold.

Sassy rolled her eyes. "Of course I do." She displayed the zip locked bag of sliced cucumbers. "But how do I get him to eat one?"

"Did you think of going up to him and offering him one?"

"I can't do that?"

"Why not?"

"Because..." she scrabbled for an excuse. "What if he doesn't want any?"

Dana held up her hands. "Just don't worry about that until he actually refuses."

"What if he's allergic--"

"Enough, Sassy. Anyhow, this phone call is yours."

"Wha--?"

Dana tossed her an earpiece and took the line off hold.

"Um, Helpdesk, this is Sassy?"

"Uh, Hello?" It was Adel. Sassy scowled at Dana. She wasn't ready to execute her plan. She needed psyching up. "What happened to the other girl?" he asked.

"What? Dana?"

Dana waved her hands in denial at Sassy then skipped out of the office, leaving Sassy on her own. "Um, she accidentally spilled something on her and had to go get it cleaned up. Can I help you?"

He sighed. "Promise you won't laugh? I've got little sheep eating the icons on my desktop."

Silence.

"Sassy?"

"Okay..." Sheep? "I'm not sure what you're talking about."

"I guess it's something you've got to come and see."

Fair enough. "I'll be down right away."

Dana's arm came around the edge of the doorway and pointed desperately at the bag of cucumbers Sassy had dropped on the desk.

As Sassy left, Dana slunk back into the office and got back to answering phone calls.

* * *

Sassy knocked on the edge of the cubicle, being very careful about the loose panel. It had been repaired since yesterday, but was it any more stable? "Hi," she said, munching on a slice of cucumber. Dana had explained in this morning's phone call that both of them had to eat the cucumber. Sassy didn't mind, but would Adel partake? "What's this about sheep?"

Adel stood in the far corner of his cubicle and pointed to the monitor. Sassy had a look. Sure enough, there were little animated sheep wandering around the desktop, munching on files and tearing off the wallpaper. "I don't know how it got there," he confessed. "I swear I didn't download anything from the internet, or click on any strange icons or anything. I logged in and five minutes later they showed up. Every time I clicked on one to drag it to the trash can, it'd just climb back out."

Sassy knew exactly what it was and who had put the harmless little applet on his computer. She didn't know if she should curse or thank Dana for her interference. "But your printers are working, right?"

"I don't know," Adel replied, a touch of worry in his voice. "I can't open the file."

Uh oh. "Why not?"

Adel looked bashful. "The sheep ate the icon."

Sassy turned away so Adel couldn't see her fail to suppress a smile. After she stalled for recovery time by wiggling the mouse and chasing a few of the sheep, she straightened and picked a cucumber out of the bag. She held it out to Adel. "Don't worry. Your document is safe. Have some cucumber while I fix this little problem."

He looked at it, at her, then back to the cucumber. She offered it again with an encouraging nod. After a moment's hesitation, he took it and bit down.

Triumph.

Sassy turned back to the computer with little seedlings of joy in her heart. She pulled up the Task Manager and killed off the little sheep. Then she scanned the computer for any remaining traces of sheep.exe that Dana may have left behind. As cute as it was, she didn't want to have to come back to fix the same problem again. She had a reputation to protect.

"There, all clean."

Adel sighed with relief. "Thank God. I've got a big presentation in an hour, but I don't know if it's going to work out. Your managers are idiots and I'm surprised their bookkeeping hasn't been called into account before."

Sassy stared at him for a moment. He'd never been this candid with her before, especially about office politics. "Um, they're not really my managers. I'm a contractor."

He looked at her, his eyes narrowing. "So you have no loyalty to this company?"

She shook her head. "Not really. I'm just filling in between gigs. Even though I've got several degrees in CS and lots of experience in the industry, it's still a tight market, even years after the DotCom Crash." Sassy found herself wanting to tell him everything. "Helpdesk is bottom of the totem pole and the pay, the hours and working conditions are shocking. Still, it's better than nothing and I've got rent to pay."

"When's your contract up?"

"Two months."

"You gonna renew?"

"Not if I've got something better lined up."

"Good. I'm certain this branch is going to close by the end of the year, unless it collapses on itself first. Your managers are real assholes. If I wasn't in my boss' bad books back home, I wouldn't be out here."

"What'd you do?"

Adel's company phone rang. He picked it up. While he spoke to someone on the other end, Sassy picked up her bag of cucumbers. She lifted one and munched it.

"*Stront!*" Adel cursed as he slammed down the phone. "Your asshole managers have moved the meeting up half an hour. I'm not going to be ready."

Sassy said a naughty word of her own. "We were supposed to have that set up this morning. That's why I came in early."

He gestured to her bag of cucumbers. "Is that why you're still eating breakfast?"

Sassy lifted the bag. "What? This? No. But yes, we often eat breakfast and lunch at the desk, and we'd probably eat dinner too, but we have a firm policy to not answer phones after five pm, otherwise we'd be here all night. Really, it's unfair for all the permanent staff to have to work overtime, though they're only allowed so many hours, and if they go over, they don't get paid. That's why I'm glad I'm a contractor." She lifted the bag again. For some reason, she had to tell him all about her cucumbers. "See, this is really the result of a magic spell. Last night Dana helped me make this spell with this cucumber and then I had to slice it up this morning and I had to make sure you ate some and then--"

Adel stared at her with growing horror. "You made me do WHAT?" He backed away from Sassy. "What's really in that?"

"Oh, no," she said, trying to calm him. "It's just cucumber, and a little bit of butter. I didn't even salt it because Dana told me not to, but I did sprinkle a bit of salt under my bed and--"

"You know, you're creeping me out."

"Really, it's okay. It's nothing bad. It's just a love spell."

"A love spell?"

"See, I love you and I want you to love me too, but, oh dear, I don't think it's working, because you're looking at me in a funny way and..." she swallowed. "You don't look like you love me."

He kept his distance and his tongue. She stepped forward and he scooted back. "Look, I thought you were okay, but now you're being scary. Women your age always go scary."

Sassy gasped. "Women my age? What's that's supposed to mean?"

"That's the way you go. You spend your twenties all Career-Bitch, eating guys like us for lunch, and then when you start getting old and desperate, you go strange. You resort to these little games and dances to try and trick us into," he crouched his fingers in quotation marks, "into 'Relationships' like it's some sort of competition--"

"It is a competition!" She crouched her own fingers, "'Women my age' who are single and lonely try looking for a decent guy to share the rest of our lives with, but you are all so narrow-minded and shallow and stuck-up. You look at us and only see dried-up old 'Career-Bitches' who aren't worth a second look just because we've been around the block a few times. Oh, no!" she shrilled, shaking her finger in his face, "instead, you, dried-up old career bastards that you are, you go chasing the much-younger women, the sweet little trophy-wives with their smooth skin and tight butts and inexperienced little bubble-heads."

Her voice had raised enough to draw the attention of the lemmings in the other cubicles. They lifted their eyes above the top of the walls separating them to see what all the noise was. Sassy scowled them down and they retreated back into the clandestinity of their cells.

Meanwhile, she never lost a beat. "See, we don't have a chance. You take one look at them, and all your blood goes south, and you end up thinking with the wrong head. Not once do you ever stop to consider that 'women my age' have personality and experience. We're good for more than just looking good on your arm and a tumble in bed. We're interesting. We've got good conversation. And a woman reaches her sexual peak in her thirties."

Adel folded his arms. "So, tell me, Miss Good Conversation, does it last well into your forties as well?"

That stung. "I am not in my forties!" She gestured at him. "Like you can talk!" She hesitated. "How old are you, anyway?"

He told her.

"Huh. You're older than I am. By two years!" She shook twin fingers in his face. "Two years! In high school, you would have looked at me and dismissed me as too young."

He spread his arms. "At our age, that sort of age difference doesn't matter."

"Maybe not two years, but twenty years does. Forget the little girls and try dating women your own age."

His phone rang, adding to the tension in the air between them. Adel lifted the receiver, shouted, "Frack off!" into it and slammed it back down. He turned his attention back to Sassy. "In case you forgot, I don't date anyone! I'm not here long enough."

"You're not here long enough for an evening over drinks? You can't enjoy one night out?" What kind of person would be so afraid of breaking up they wouldn't even go out once?

"It wouldn't be just an evening over drinks, would it? If the first date went well, you'd want a second, possibly dinner. And they maybe a

third, and a fourth, assuming all went well. If it doesn't go well, you'll get all strange and bitter and I'll have to worry about more little sheep running about my computer, or worse. That's assuming things don't work."

"But they might work," she replied, wistfully.

"That's what I'm afraid of. But it doesn't matter. Sooner or later, you're going to get a broken heart, and I don't want to have to deal with that."

Sassy's heart was breaking already. "But can't we try?"

"So where does it end?"

"It doesn't have to end," Sassy insisted.

"It always ends. I'm only here for a few months more..."

"So am I."

He shook his head. "No, I'm going back to Europe after this. And after that? Hong Kong, Perth, maybe Los Angeles. Always a few months here and there. Too short for a proper relationship, and too long to be away if I had one back home."

"What if I followed you?"

"And where would you get the money for that? You wouldn't be around long enough to hold a decent job."

Sassy felt increasingly frustrated. Why did he have to push her away so hard? "I work in the computer industry. There's little contracts all over the world I could pick up or..."

"There's no chance you'd pick up a contract that started and ended the same time mine did."

"...Or I could get a telecommuting job. My last permanent position involved mostly telecommuting. I'm sure I could find another."

"Oh really? Then why are you stuck working a short-term help desk contract when you could be in a permanent telecommuting job?"

Sassy didn't answer right away. Her first instinct was to blurt out the first thing on her mind, but that's what she'd been doing for the past five minutes. Why was she being so candid with him? She took a deep breath and confessed the truth. "Because if I took a permanent job that meant I'd be home all the time, I'd never get out and I'd never meet anyone to spend the rest of my life with.

It's true 'women my age' get like this, but that's only because our clocks run out sooner. And when that ticking starts slowing down, we become aware of our mortality. At least we recognize it early enough that we can do something about it... unlike men, where you wake up with only five, maybe ten years left to your life. You're old and wrinkled and alone, and you're going to die that way. Who'll miss you? Who'll mourn you? You don't have any sense of mortality until it's too late. And what about children? Unless you've got a lot of money, no fertile woman's gonna look twice at a bitter old bachelor."

"I never said anything about children."

"Better say something now, because by the time you think of it on your own, it'll be too late."

Dana popped her head around the edge of the cubicle. To Adel, she said, "I'm not the kind to frack off." She grabbed Sassy's arm. "You're needed." As she pulled Sassy away, she promised, "You can flirt with him later."

Sassy glanced back at Adel. Adel refused to look at her. He folded his arms and turned to stare out the window.

* * *

"Who's at the desk?" Sassy asked.

"No one." Dana did not release Sassy's arm until they were back at the office where the phone was already ringing. Dana grabbed the call and while she was dealing with that, the other line rang. Sassy picked up the phone. "Helpdesk, this is Sassy." She listened to the plaintiff on the other end. "Mm hmm... mm hmm... You know, Phillipa," she said, interrupting the accountant, "I've told you several times that the reason you can't find your documents is because of your stupid little naming convention. I've told you time and time again that you shouldn't use dates to name your documents and if you must, you can't use backslashes to separate the numbers. That's for separating subdirectories." Phillipa couldn't get a word in. "Last time, I came down there and spent half an hour sorting everything out. Now you've screwed it up again. You can sort it out yourself this time, and if you weren't paying attention last time, I'm certainly not helping you now, and if I ever get another phone call from you about this, I'm never going to help you with anything ever again!"

She hung up without saying goodbye.

Dana, who'd long ago terminated her call, stared at Sassy with a funny look. "What's gotten into you?"

Sassy told her, at length. She told her about how Adel discovered the incompetency of the managers, and about her contract, and then about the spell - though she didn't mean to - and how he called her old, and she called him shallow, and how if he didn't get his head out of his butt he'd find himself old and alone...

"Sassy?"

"And really, it was all his fault for his stupid policy of never even dating, much less getting involved..."

"Sassy?"

She rambled on. "And it was a shame he wasn't doing anything to secure his future..."

"Sassy!"

"Hmm?"

"Shut up."

"Oh." She didn't realize how much she'd been talking.

The phone rang. Dana picked it up then hung up. Picking up her line again, she put it on hold and did the same to Sassy's. Anyone calling would get a busy signal.

Undisturbed, Dana turned her thoughts to Sassy's problems, or rather, problem.

"You must have messed up the spell."

"What?" gasped Sassy. "How could I? You were guiding me every step of the way."

"Did you use real salt?"

Sassy rolled her eyes. "What other kind is there?"

"Low-sodium salt substitute."

Sassy waved her hand. "That's for old people. And yes, it was real salt."

"The paper was green?"

"Yes, and I guarantee his hair and my hair really belonged to us and that was really a cucumber."

"And the butter?"

"Was really.... Oh no," Sassy groaned.

Dana groaned too. "Don't tell me you used margarine."

"I didn't know there was a difference!"

"If you'd ever baked cookies, you'd know."

Sassy dropped her forehead into her palm. "Now I've totally screwed up."

"Not completely. You seem to have discovered a rather effective truth-telling spell."

"Ha, ha," sneered Sassy. "Not only did I ruin my chances with Adel, but might have ruined his job as well.

He's got that meeting in half an hour..." She smacked her forehead. "...that I've gotta set up!" Sassy said a dirty word and bolted to her feet.

"Spells can be reversed," Dana called after her as she headed off to the conference room to ensure that the resident computer was networked properly and that it worked through the overhead projector.

To Sassy's relief, everything worked fine first time. As she logged out of the computer, Adel showed up. Sassy stood and fiddled nervously with her fingers. "Look," she began, "I'm sorry. This was all my fault..."

Adel put up his hand. "How about we not talk to each other for a while?"

"But..."

He hushed her again. "You're going to be strange and I've got more important things to do right now than put up with a strange woman. I don't need complications in my life and you are a complication."

"It doesn't have to be complicated."

Adel logged into the computer. "There is no such thing as an uncomplicated relationship." He watched as everything he did on the little box was projected on the overhead screen for all to see.

Sassy wrapped her arms about her body. "My parents had an uncomplicated relationship."

While he waited for the computer to log in, he pointed a finger at Sassy. "You know, if it wasn't for your strangeness and your little hocus pocus, we'd not be having this conversation. We'd be trading some awkward dialogue while I ignored you and you sighed wistfully with unrequited feelings."

"And none of us would be happy," she pointed out.

Adel turned his back and pulled up his presentation on the computer and initiated a test run. "I was perfectly happy before."

"No you weren't. You were afraid. And so you hid. You'd hide and not come out at all to enjoy the sunshine."

Adel rolled his eyes. "What are you talking about?"

"I'm talking about you not even going out to have a little fun. You are so worried about the risk of just liking someone, never mind loving someone, that you can't even go out and have a casual drink after work in case it might lead to marriage, and gosh-darn-it, if you didn't leave your tuxedo in your other pants."

"Do you know how ridiculous that sounds?"

Sassy planted her fists on her hips. "It sounds pretty ridiculous to me." Honestly, he was as bad as some of the women Sassy knew, who assumed just because you had a single date, you were practically engaged. Polite girls waited at least three dates.

Before she could point out the errors in his logic, the conference room door opened and a couple of accountants arrived five minutes early for the meeting. Knowing she was still under the influence of the spell, Sassy made a hasty exit, not even saying hello to anyone else, lest her garrulousness got her in trouble.

As she departed, she took a vindictive little satisfaction that the spell hadn't worn off Adel either, and she wished him the full effect of it for the next half hour.

* * *

By the time she returned to Dana and spilled out the story in between some far-too-honest helpdesk calls, Sassy's vindictiveness eased. Adel was European and had that Continental habit of not sharing one's inner thoughts.

The more she thought about it, the worse she felt.

"He's going to lay it out and tell it like it is and he's not going to pull any punches, isn't he?" she confessed to Dana.

Dana leaned on her arm and played with the phone cord on her desk. "Perhaps that's a good thing. Maybe the PTBs need to hear honesty like that."

Sassy groaned. "There's honesty and then there's a brutal knife to the chest."

"Well," Dana said with a shrug, "That's that, I guess."

Sassy's head sank down to the desk and she whimpered. "I've really screwed things up. He called me strange." She sat up. "But I'm not. I can't help it if I can see things clearer than he can."

"Oh, really? So what's your next move, Miss Unstrange Clearthoughts?"

"Oh, what next move? It's over. I've proven myself an idiot."

Dana chuckled. "You give up too easily."

"It's not giving up when it's the end of the road."

"Well, then, I guess if that's that," Dana replied, tapping the side of her nose, "then the only thing left to do is apologize. After lunch."

Sassy closed her eyes and swallowed. Dana was right. Sassy may have made a fool of herself, but at least she could retain some adult dignity by apologizing.

As Sassy worked the phones throughout the rest of the morning, she noticed the gradual fading of the spell. Soon she found she could plaster the ol' telemarketer's smile to her face and deliver the professional-caliber BS that marked the skilled helpdesk tech without feeling this overwhelming need to explain exactly what an ID-10-T user error was.

Dana slipped off to lunch first on her insistence. Sassy agreed, for she felt she needed to atone for that morning.

Dana returned with a full belly, a few flowers behind her back and a mysterious smile on her face. "I brought you something." She presented the bouquet to Sassy. "But don't sniff 'em. They're for you to give to Adel."

Sassy paused with the flowers half-way to her face. "Uh, Dana, what did you do to these flowers?"

"Oh, just a little something called 'Courage'..."

Sassy held the flowers away from her face. "Not another spell!"

"It's a simple spell. One sniff will give you courage. If that's what's holding Adel back, then a little courage may help things along."

Sassy gave Dana a wan look. "I don't know if I can do this."

Dana waved her hand over the flowers until their scent, perfumery and a little acrid, drifted across Sassy's nose. Sassy screwed up her face and scratched her nose.

However, she did feel a little better. In fact, a lot better. Perhaps an apology was in order. "I see what you mean. But it won't change things between Adel and me."

Dana shrugged. "Make them change. You don't need magic. Only opportunity." With that, she shoved Dana out of the office.

As she strode to the cubicle where perhaps Adel was trying to find a box big enough to hold his personal belongings, including one pot plant, she figured this courage thing wasn't too bad.

Okay, so Adel wasn't cleaning out his desk. When Sassy arrived, he wasn't doing much of anything, just staring at the computer screen. He was startled when Sassy tapped on the partition frame.

"Hi," she said with a small smile. "I came to apologise." She handed him the flowers. "I didn't know what you liked, I thought you might think tulips twee, so I got these. They're supposed to have a nice scent, but I'm not sure."

Adel took them and inhaled, just like he was supposed to. Sassy wondered how many men Dana had affected this way.

He, too, wrinkled his nose and scratched it. "I think I would have preferred tulips. Anyhow, I'll be seeing those soon enough. My job is done; I'll be leaving at the end of the week."

"Oh," replied Sassy. What else was she going to say? For the first time since she met Adel, her tongue didn't feel awkward, nor did she feel she would stumble across any words. If only she had some to say.

Adel looked at the flowers then laid them on his desk. "Look. Don't take this the wrong way. I don't want to start another argument; I just want to set the record straight.

"I am not afraid. I'm just cautious."

Something clicked in Sassy and she saw what Dana meant. "So, are you afraid of pastrami sandwiches?"

Adel raised an eyebrow. "What are you talking about?"

"If you're not afraid of pastrami sandwiches, then you won't be afraid to try one. If you're not afraid, as you say, then you won't mind going to have lunch with a friend. Nothing implied, no agendas and I solemnly swear I will not stop to look at wedding dresses on the way there."

"I don't know if this is a good idea."

Sassy sighed. "Oh, Adel. After the morning we had, do you really think I'd try something suss? You'd see through me in an instant." She resisted the temptation to cross her fingers behind her back. "It is just lunch, and you'll be gone in a week. Nothing could possibly happen between now and then."

He gave her a shy smirk. "Perhaps you're right."

Sassy hoped she wasn't.

The End

About the author: Heidi Wessman Kneale is a writer of moderate repute. She's been writing stories for as long as she can remember. By day she works computer miracles for the local library. She understands, first-hand, the life of a woman in the IT industry and has even managed to find love there. The wrest of the time she writes books and wraises babies. Visit Heidi's website: http://members.iinet.net.au/~damian/heidikneale/

Space Opera
Science Fiction Storyline Edited by Darlene Oakley

A
Time
To Die

by Margreta J. Eubanks

Dear Readers,

    Eisodos Space Station sits at the very edge of the Milky Way Galaxy policing traffic in and out.   Commander Jonathan Aaron Carpenter and his crew of humanoids and various non-humanoids are stunned to discover a frozen human female aboard the station.

    Each writer was permitted to create their own crew and their own personalities for the various characters.   The description of the Polaxians was written by MUBS contributor Francis Tokarski.   This was the only alien "legislated." Each writer was also given leeway as to how this woman arrived, why she had been frozen in the first place and how her experience and arrival affects the people on the station and the people of earth.

    Margreta Eubanks' story "A Time to Die" presents a imaginative group of aliens to help Carpenter and his crew solve this mystery. What begins, in Carpenter's mind, as a simple negotiation turns sour as the Draconier brothers refuse to give her up and Carpenter refuses to kill her, as he is required to do by law.

Darlene Oakley
Space Adventure Editor

A Time to Die

For Heidi at Goebel Liquors, for invaluable assistance with spelling.

Stardate: 01-10-2310
Eisodos Light Side
15:00 Hours

"So tell me again, Lieutenant Squidley, why am I in full dress uniform and on my way to visit the ship of a couple of pirates?" John Carpenter, a Commander in the Navy section of the United Earth Space Forces, tugged at the cuffs of his gray and gold dress uniform jacket. He strode down the hallway leading to the myriad of docking bays on deck fifty. The bays formed a ring around the ball of the great space station, Eisodos, halving it.

"Because they're direct relations of the Polaxian Oligarchy. The Polaxian contingent that first contacted Earth fifty years ago included their mother." Squidley fingered his collar and swallowed, his gills flaring.

"I'm aware of when the Polaxians arrived, Lieutenant." Carpenter's voice matched the ice in his blue eyes.

The young lieutenant came from an amphibious race on the planet Velidia. Humanoid, Velidians had two arms, two legs, opposable thumbs, and breathed oxygen. They differed from humans in that they had gills, webbing between their digits, transparent eyelids, and pale, perpetually moist, greenish-white skin. Squidley had applied for and received Earth citizenship in order to join the prestigious fleet that controlled Eisodos and made it the "Gateway to the Milky Way."

The Global Space Exploration Agency and the Polaxians may have built Eisodos, but the Navy ran it. Carpenter had come into command of the station at the tender age of twenty-five, making him not much older than Squidley. He desired nothing more than to prove his mettle, refuting the rumors he had received his post, rather than the captaincy of a starship, because his granddaddy had discovered the Light Drive.

"Yes, sir." Squidley's voice squeaked, his gills flared even wider and his cheeks flushed a deeper shade of blue-green.

"So, they're connected Polaxian pirates, Mister Squidley. Why am I going to *their* ship? Why are they not coming to *my* office?"

Squidley squirmed even more, and Carpenter thought he might widdle down the leg of his uniform pants. The Commander ran his free hand through his thick blue-black hair ruffling his short locks into disarray. Reining in his temper he said, "Well?"

Squidley's gills flapped in rhythmic agitation. "The Draconier brothers docked their ship, last night; a modified destroyer with Altery Sector registration called *The Devil Hunter*. Has Light Drive, carries mid-level firepower and a crew of eighty-seven hands. A routine inspection discovered a cryogenically frozen adult human female stashed in a hidden chamber in the hold. They would never have found her if they hadn't had a sniffing dog with them."

Carpenter halted in mid-stride. "Wait. Wait. I'm being called down to the docks to deal with some pirate's private piece of a--"

"No, no, sir! It's not that simple, sir."

"Squidley, why aren't these brothers in the brig, their ship impounded, and the woman thawed out and in a rehab somewhere?"

"Well, that's just it, sir. The inspection crew called security. Security demanded the brothers surrender the woman and give themselves up for arrest. The Draconiers refused and drew their guns. Their communications officer got off a message to the Polaxian embassy. A lawyer and a minor Polaxian official arrived. Then, some dockside do-gooder called the press and both the Daughters of Artemis and the Sisters of Rahab. The Draconiers are holed up in the ship. Their mouthpieces are crying diplomatic immunity. Meanwhile both women's groups are demanding the woman be turned over to them and that the brothers be executed for slavery. Security is having a hard time controlling the crowds. It's a circus, sir."

Carpenter muttered a piece of profanity not in keeping with his rank and uniform. "Diplomats and lawyers. Daughters and Sisters. That means both

Heidi Wulfsdottir and Marguerite the Red are there. This isn't a circus, Squidley, it's a fliggering disaster."

"Yes, sir." Squidley pulled at his collar once again. "Uh, sir, I also have it on good authority that there's been a threat from the Draconiers to blow the dock."

Carpenter's mouth dried and his blood dropped clear to the soles of his spit-shined black boots. If the Draconiers fired up *The Devil Hunter* and pulled away without undocking the resulting hole in the space station would blow everything from that bay out into the vacuum of space, weakening the rest of the bays and throwing the rotation of the station off. Countless lives would be lost.

"They can't be serious," he breathed. "If they do that, not even the *Nana-Naga-Nagagda* of Polaxia could help them."

"I spoke with Sergeant Jalicand himself, sir. His comments required heavy editing, but the gist was unmistakable. The Draconiers have agreed to meet with you, and only you, in the captain's cabin of *The Devil Hunter*."

Carpenter resumed striding toward the docks. He pressed the node in his neck containing the implant that allowed him to communicate via-cranial with the Eisodos central computer. "Get me all the information you can on the Draconier brothers, now." He turned to speak to Squidley. "Have they taken any individual hostages?"

"Not at this time, sir."

"Of course not. Why would they have to? They've got the whole of Eisodos in their hands."

Eisodos Central downloaded to Carpenter's brain, the comp's voice ringing inside his head. "Draconier, Courvoisier Walter and Draconier, Drambuie Scott. Twins. Born 23:56 and 23:59, June 6, 2290, Draconier State House, Polaxia. Mother: Elantessa Iellonia Marquedia Draconier. Father: Aidan Mallory. No pictures available. Tutored through elementary and secondary years. Enrolled at Cambridge University, Earth 2308. Expelled later that same year for misconduct. No details available. Purchased ship from Altery Shipyards June 6, 2309. Ship refitted and reregistered under the name *The Devil Hunter* August 12, 2309. Letters of marque and reprisal issued from Altery government August 12, 2309. Occupation: privateers. While the brothers have a reputation for drinking, brawling and womanizing, no illegal ties can be attributed to them, and there are no arrests for major crimes on their record. Docked in bay 117, Eisodos Space Station."

"Let's hope they stay there," Carpenter muttered. "Wonderful. I've got the Hardy Boys on steroids, the women's rights leader, the union organizer for prostitutes, and the whole government of Polaxia duking it out in my docking bay. Add the press and with any luck this could turn into the first Interstellar War."

"Do you think so, sir?" asked Squidley, gills working overtime.

Carpenter's icy blues shot laser beams at his lieutenant and any color left in the boy's face melted away.

"Forget I said that, sir."

They rounded the corner to the bay and came to a sudden halt.

"Sweet, suffering Vespa," Carpenter swore. "I don't believe it!"

The bay resembled a twentieth century can of sardines. People stood shoulder-to-shoulder, blocking forward movement. Chanting rose above the crowd but neither Carpenter nor Squidley could make out the words. Image scanners clicked as the reporters shouted questions. The antsy crowd shuddered and swayed to any sound or any shift in the raucous voices.

Carpenter called Eisodos Central again. "Get any off duty or low priority security down to bay 117. Issue standard riot gear, stun sticks and non-lethal wide-spray stun guns. Institute a curfew effective now. No one is allowed on the promenade without a written clearance. Rescind all passes and shore leaves. All personnel are to return to their ships. Patch me through to the Captain of *The Rising Dragon*."

Yellow lights flashed overhead and a computerized female voice bellowed instructions, which were simultaneously translated into every language and dialect, for the dockside to be cleared. The crowd buzzed like hornets, tentative at first, then louder and more aggressive as the security teams appeared.

Squidley and Carpenter elbowed their way through the morass, heading toward *The Devil Hunter's* docking ramp. Bodies shoved between them, forcing them apart. Carpenter bullied his way to the front of the mass. When Carpenter broke though the last line of people he almost wished he could turn and go back.

Marguerite the Red stood on a stack of cargo boxes, screaming exhortations to the prostitutes present to take up arms and protect themselves. The petite red-head wore her trademark red dress. Well-cut, tailored and expensive, it covered a decent amount of her, while still managing to convey an air of availability. Her ladies followed her instructions, picking up any loose item that came to hand and flinging it at anything wearing a security uniform. Carpenter ducked as a nasty-looking cargo hook flew his way.

The well-stacked bulk of Heidi Wulfsdottir also mounted a crate. Heidi's blue eyes shone with fervor as she led her portion of the crowd in the old Earth protest hymn "We Shall Overcome." Six feet tall, her long white dress made her look big. Not fat, but rather a tower of massive, well-curved muscle. Her fair hair sat dressed high upon her head in an upswept Grecian style.

When the voice of the warship's Captain echoed in his head Carpenter didn't recognize it as outside the cacophony around him.

"I beg your pardon, Captain. Would you repeat that please?"

"I said *The Rising Dragon.* This is Naismith. What in Hades is going on in there, John?" Captain Lois Naismith's voice held puzzlement. "We've been monitoring transmissions. That Altery ship has been banging off coded stream in the direction of Polaxia for hours now."

"Lois, I'm requesting you block those radio messages. I'm also requesting you position *The Dragon* behind *The Devil Hunter,* bring all your guns to bear on her and change your ship's status to yellow alert."

After a pause Naismith asked, "Would you care to elaborate, John?"

"I can't at the moment. Let's just say I've got a situation here."

A longer, more pregnant pause rang in his head. Then Lois Naismith said, "All right, John. I'll do what you ask. But if you call back asking me to fire on that vessel, I may not be able to accommodate you."

"Understood. Let's just pray to God I don't have to do that. Carpenter out."

"Naismith out. Good luck, John."

"I'm going to need it," Carpenter muttered as the computer cut the connection.

"Squidley! Lieutenant Eustace B. Squidley, report!"

A knot in the crowd shifted, heaved and vomited out his lieutenant. Squidley had torn the gold braid and gray sleeve of his uniform coat. A goose egg bulged above his left eyebrow and his sea-green hair stood on end. His shining eyes and victorious grin made Carpenter grin in return.

"Here, Commander!" he shouted.

"Let's move, Squidley. Try to keep up."

"Yes, sir," the boy huffed as he fell in beside Carpenter.

They had almost made it to the ramp when a voice rang out, "Carpenter! Commander Carpenter!"

Carpenter turned back to face Heidi Wulfsdottir and Marguerite the Red. Two beautiful, intelligent, passionate women committed to the causes they championed. For a brief moment Carpenter wondered what it would be like to have them both in bed at the same time. He chivvied his randy thoughts into line.

"Ladies," he acknowledged.

"Are you going in there?" Marguerite demanded.

"I have been invited to speak with the Draconier brothers in their cabin."

"We want to go in with you." Heidi's hands rested defiantly on her hips. "A woman has been victimized here. She deserves to be represented by members of her own sex."

"Much as I agree with you, Heidi," Carpenter said, "It's not up to me."

"Of course it's up to you," Marguerite snapped. "You're the station commander."

"Squidley, find me Sergeant Jalicand. Yesterday."

"Aye, aye, sir!"

"Marguerite, I may be commander, I can't take civilians into a dangerous situation. You know that."

Jalicand chose that moment to appear.

Riposte Jalicand measured five feet two inches with hair the same flaming red as Marguerite's. His stature defied the traditional expectations for a top security operative, but Carpenter had learned on the exercise mat that fast, deadly Rip deserved his name.

"Commander," he drawled. "How good of you to come."

"Sergeant," Carpenter kept his tone level and pleasant. "Next time, I expect you to meet me. Don't make me send my aide looking for you again or you'll be standing watch over the biowaste recycling compound wearing a seaman's bars. Understood? Give me your cuffs."

Jalicand raised his eyebrows and relinquished his flexcuffs. "Aye, aye, sir."

Before either woman could bat an eyelash Carpenter seized Marguerite's left hand and attached it to Lieutenant Squidley's right wrist. Squidley's mouth dropped in surprise. Marguerite's face turned as scarlet as her hair.

Heidi turned to run, but Jalicand stuck out a casual foot and tripped her. She fell hard, her white gown riding up to reveal voluptuous legs. Rip put his knee in the small of her back, pulled her arms behind her and prised her wrists in one of his deft hands. Holding up the other, he snapped his fingers. One of his men tossed him another set of cuffs and he fastened Heidi's wrist to his. Hauling her to her feet, Rip glanced at Carpenter and grinned.

"Talk about your wildest dreams," he said.

"You can't do this!" Heidi screamed.

"Oh, but I can. And I have. Book 'em on a 24-hour

hold, then release them on their own recognizance."

"Aye, aye, sir." Jalicand gave Heidi a gentle shove. "Come along, darlin'. It's just you and me now."

Heidi set her bulk against him trying to force him to drag her. Rip laughed, snaked an arm around her waist and threw her over his shoulder like a bag of flour. He staggered a little under her weight, but kept his feet and carried her away despite the blows from her free hand that pummeled his back.

Squidley was having his own battles with his quarry as Marguerite swung and_caught his cheekbone, sending his head rocking back. At last he wrestled her over his shoulder in imitation of Sergeant Jalicand. As he staggered off with his burden, Carpenter called after them, "Be gentle with him, Marguerite. It's his first time."

The swearing that drifted back to him would have done credit to any of his sailors. Laughter caught his attention and Carpenter swung back to face the loading ramp to *The Devil Hunter*. A middle-aged man with curly blond hair, a merry face and cornflower blue eyes, dressed in a white, full-sleeved shirt and a Stuarttartan kilt stood on the ramp, cradling a long energy rifle.

"Now you've gone and done it, laddie," the man chuckled. "Those two'll have your guts for garters and your poor lads will see no fine lovin' for months on end."

"You're on my dock with a weapon," Carpenter snapped, stepping forward. "I'll thank you to stand down and hand it over."

The weapon came around and pointed square at Carpenter's middle.

"No, lad," the man said, joviality gone. "I'm no' on your dock, I'm on the ramp of *The Devil Hunter*. And that's Polaxian ground."

"I thought you hailed from Altery."

"Aye, we do. But you see, lad, there's a dear outstandin' treaty twixt the two. I know. I helped write it."

"Your Captain wanted to speak to me. Here I am."

The Scotsman laughed. "Aye. That you are, lad. I suppose I'd best be escortin' you in. Some of the crew are all for slittin' your weasand, turnin' tail and runnin' for the deep black of space."

"You pull out of here, and you'd best not leave me standing. If you do, I'll hunt you down and kill you every last mother's son of you."

The man laughed again and motioned Carpenter forward. "I believe you would, lad. I believe you would."

Carpenter took a deep breath as he followed the Scot into the bowels of the ship. Unlike many privateers and merchantmen, the halls of *The Devil Hunter* held no debris, and her metal walls gleamed with care and polish.

"You run a tight ship here."

"Aye, that we do." The Scotsman's voice oozed pride. "Master Couv will no' stand for slackin', and Black Annie what runs the sweepers is a holy terror."

They saw nothing and no one on their way. Angry voices thick with a Scots burr came from behind a real Earth oak door that Carpenter assumed led to the Captain's cabin.

"Burn it, Dram, there's a full warship parked behind us with all her guns pointed at our backside!"

"No, Couv, I had na noticed!"

"The old man is going to kill us! That's if Mummy dearest doesn't get there first! You're going to have to give it up!"

"No! I will na let..."

The voice trailed off as the Scotsman tapped an intercom and cleared his throat. Grinning he said, "If you'd been half an hour earlier, you'd have heard the sounds of fists meetin' flesh as well as ah that." He raised his voice. "Permission to enter."

Hurried sounds of movement scraped behind the door, then a voice said, "Come."

"I should have such luck," the Scotsman muttered. He threw wide the door and announced, "Jonathan Aaron Carpenter, Commander of the Space Station Eisodos."

Carpenter stepped through the door into a room where rampant hedonism reigned. Thick furs scattered over heavy patterned rugs of the finest Salisian spider silk covered the cabin floor. The walls paneled in unique Polaxian *llallik* wood, their gold carried over by a massive carved desk of the same material. A rare print of ancient Earth artist Frank Frazetta's eerie work "The Death Dealer" hung framed on the wall behind it, the red eyes of its central figure boring into the observer. Beside it hung the head of some huge bovine creature, its wicked spreading horns

stained with what appeared to be dried blood.

The linens and blankets covering the Captain's bunk, twice the size of Carpenter's own sleeping space cost more than he made in a year. The pillows looked so deep they could swallow a man whole and Carpenter longed to bury himself in them. A door beside the bunk had to lead to a private head. The subtle and indirect lighting gave one the feeling of firelight or candle flame.

A framed holograph of a Polaxian woman occupied a small place on the almost Spartan desktop. Her tall slender figure had transparent skin which showed the delicate network of violet and green arteries and veins below it. Her hairless head held an eyeless blood red oval swirling with whirlpools and tiny lightning bolts like an eerie storm-tossed sea. The floor length dress she wore of interlinked greenish Polaxian bio-steel rings accentuated the image of the sea developing in his mind.

The only other decorations sat on the opposite corner--a squat ugly figure, carved in sulfurous red gemstone, whose pendulous curves and rigid member proclaimed it a hermaphroditic fertility deity.

A dagger whose undulating blade slithered into a handle shaped like a curvaceous woman framed by a hilt made of spreading gold wings rested beside the unpleasant little idol.

With difficulty Carpenter drew his attention from the sensual surroundings to the men inhabiting it. One word described them: Flamboyant. Since they sat, he had a hard time estimating their height. Carpenter thought perhaps six foot one or two, taller than his own five foot eleven. While they must have received their stature, their cotton candy blue hair, and their metallic silver eyes from their Polaxian mother, they got their figure from their Earthen father. He had been built for fighting, sleek, and broad-shouldered with compact, massed muscle. Despite their unusual coloring, nothing about them spoke of effeminate. Square-jawed and masculine their patrician facial features gave no clue to their thoughts.

One man wore unrelieved black. He sat behind the desk, the fingers of his hands laced together lying on the desktop. Longish hair stood around his face in spikes and splinters. His expression of icy disdain challenged the world around him. A rakish black eye patch covered his left eye. A heavy gold chain holding a blue-green Polaxian naming stone swung from around his neck.

His counterpart sat offset, his feet with their calf-high glossy black boots perched, in defiance of cleanliness and good manners, on the desktop. His arms were folded across his chest, and he wore clothes of deep hunter green. Strands of uneven and shaggy hair fell across his restless silver eyes. It complimented his smoldering, sullen, handsome face. His stone hung on a shiny silver chain. A pair of high firepower blasters sat on his hips, and a huge sword, made in the ancient earthen heavy broadsword fashion, rested against the wall close to his left hand.

With a confidence he didn't feel Carpenter started the dialogue. "One of you is the Captain, I presume."

The man in black inclined his head. "Captain Courvoisier Draconier. My brother, and second in command, Drambuie Draconier." The burr had vanished into a less definable accent. Despite its uncanny, static-like resonance, the Captain's voice had a hypnotic quality that left Carpenter wrapped in an eerie sense of reassurance and comfort.

Shaking off the reaction, Carpenter stepped forward, placed his hands on the desktop and leaned into the other man's space. "Let's have something understood from the beginning, Captain. There's an eighty thousand ton warship sitting behind you with its guns fixed on you. If your engineer so much as breathes on the controls, you're going to be missing the entire back half of this ship. Have I made myself clear?"

"Crystalline, Commander. Now let me help *you* to understand something. If our coded broadcasts are more than an hour late or this ship is fired upon, the entire fleet of Polaxia will be enroute to disassemble what they helped assemble twenty-five years ago."

Carpenter glowered and tapped his link. "Carpenter to *The Rising Dragon*."

"*Dragon* here. Go ahead, sir."

"Request that you discontinue blocking transmissions from *The Devil Hunter*."

"Acknowledged. Anything else, Commander?"

"Not at this time. Carpenter out."

The brothers exchanged a glance and Carpenter noticed the tension ease between them. He didn't like what he saw. He wanted them off-balance and uncertain. It gave him the advantage in the verbal sparring.

"Gentlemen," he said. "Let's be blunt. You're breaking the law."

Couv cocked his head. "Oh? In what way?"

"You're holding an adult human female in cryo freeze, Captain."

"My legal counsel informs me that said person can be construed as spoils of war, Commander."

"Dragon dung."

"I beg your pardon?"

"You heard me. The laws of Earth, Polaxia and Eisodos Station state that no sentient being, human or alien, of any gender or sexual orientation may be held in a cryogenic state against their will or for illegal or immoral purposes."

Couv sighed. "I assure you, Commander, the woman is not being held against her will. Nor is she being held for immoral purposes."

"Good. That just leaves illegal." Carpenter shook his head. "Listen, all you boys have to do is surrender. Let us thaw the woman and put her in rehab. With your lawyers, money and connections you won't get more than a slap on the hand."

Consideration crossed Courvoisier's face until Drambuie said in a low warning tone, "Couv, don't."

Couv snorted, tossed his head and looked away. Carpenter persisted.

"Why would the two of you and the Polaxian government be willing to go to war for this woman?"

Couv leaned back in his chair and ran his hand through his hair in a quick impatient gesture that left it even more spiked. "We're going to have to tell him, Dram. There's nothing else for it."

Dram hit his leg with his fist. "No good will come of it."

"Our back is against the wall, brother."

Dram hung his head. He pinched the bridge of his nose between his thumb and forefinger as if his head ached. Then he swung his feet to the floor and stood. "All right. I'll see to waking her. We can use the cell in the brig with the force field across the door." He turned to Carpenter. "We had to put her in cryo, Commander. For her safety as well as our own. Believe me when I say, the

last thing I want to do is hurt this woman."

Dram stalked from the room, anger and more than a little fear written in his walk.

"It's true, Commander," Couv said as they watched him vanish through the door. "We froze her for everyone's protection."

"I find that hard to believe."

"You'll believe it in a few minutes, Commander."

Courvoisier opened a drawer in the desk, pulled out a bottle of his namesake, set it and two snifters on the desktop. He manhandled his brother's chair over the *llallik* wood surface, shoving it toward Carpenter.

"May I offer you a drink, Commander," he asked.

Carpenter seated himself. "Don't mind if I do."

They sat in companionable silence. Carpenter savored the burn of the fine liquor as it slid down his throat. "You know, without the threats and the guns and the chest beating, I'd almost consider this a courtesy call."

Couv sighed. "True. The circumstances are less than amenable."

A hidden intercom rang with Dram's voice. "Brig to Captain. She's starting to come around, Couv. Get him down here. He might as well see the worst. Besides I'm not too sure how long I can hold her."

They rose. As Couv Draconier stood, the set of swords he wore, hidden by the desk, came into view. A long katana rested near his right hand. An *Om-Gladiv-Zung,* the legendary Polaxian blitzsword, hung at his left. Carpenter sat the remains of his brandy on the desktop when Couv suggested, "You ought to finish it. When this is over you'll wish you had."

Carpenter slugged down the liquor with more haste than its quality deserved. He set the empty snifter next to the small, repulsive god.

Couv swept his hand toward the door. "After you, Commander."

Carpenter followed Couv through the corridors of the ship. The clean lines and functional layout of the vessel impressed him. They met an eclectic crew: Humans dressed in coveralls; eerie Polaxians, wearing their wealth on their persons in clothing made of bio-steel rings, a haunting jingling sound following them as they walked; and, even an insectoid Zhary with repair equipment nestled in its chitin clad "hands." Most of the crew greeted their Captain

and his "guest" with respectful nods and acknowledgments.

A willowy woman with black hair, midnight eyes and a face like an Andalusian Madonna fixed on Draconier and Carpenter as they passed. Her glare reminded Carpenter of the raging bonfires during summer fishing trips to his grandfather's estate. Couv met the hatred in her scowl with a glacial indifference, sweeping by her without so much as a backward glance.

A few steps past the woman Couv addressed Carpenter in a voice loud enough to carry through the corridor. "Don't mind Annie, Commander. She and my brother were...intimates. She's lost both money and face with her shipmates now that his interests have, shall we say, moved on."

"You took long enough," Dram complained as they arrived outside the cell. A slight distortion and a low humming sound indicated an active force field.

"Where is she?" The slight note of panic in Couv's voice surprised Carpenter.
"Right here." Dram reached behind him with gentle hands and drew out the tiny, trembling form of the woman.

For a moment Carpenter thought they'd been lying to him, that they not a woman, but a child. Rage swept through him. The woman cried out in terror and threw herself against Dram's massive body. Kneeling, he comforted her with his enormous arms. The argent gaze he flashed Carpenter over the woman's shoulder held a fierce and molten fury.

"Get him out, Couv," he snapped. "Now! Before I canna handle the temptation to kill the both of you."

Couv laid a hand on Carpenter's shoulder, but the Commander shrugged it off. He sucked in a deep breath and tamped down his emotions to a null state. As his feelings calmed so did the woman. An adult woman, he noted, short of stature, but with soft round breasts and wide sweet hips. A damp Rapunzelian braid of winter white hair slithered down her back to coil in a layer at her feet.

Carpenter found her state of undress distracting. "Get something on her," he demanded.

"Will na do any good," Dram Draconier's breathing quickened once more and his words slurred. A torrid, dreamy look came into his silver eyes. "She can skinny out of clothes faster than a two-year-old."

Taking off his green coat and slinging it over the woman's shoulders he murmured, "Shh, Dama. It's ah right. I'm here..." His words trailed off into a feral moan as the woman reached up, cupped her hands around his face and drew his mouth down to hers.

Carpenter closed his eyes, turned his head to the side and bit off a sharp descriptive epithet.

"You know what she is?" Couv's ashen voice made Carpenter visualize barren worlds charred to cinders. "A high-level telepath/empath. Both receives and sends."

When he didn't respond, Couv continued his recitation in his distant voice ignoring the sounds and sighs coming from the cell. "She's an unregistered, untrained, unlicensed psychic. Do you understand now why we had to put her into a frozen state?"

Still, Carpenter remained silent.

"Dinna ya see! She's designed to fasten on to whatever is uppermost in a person's subconscious mind. With Dram it's sex. When she stood next to me the end result was two crewmen in the dispensary and a third buried in space. Stand her next to you, Commander, and God knows what you'll get. We froze her and made for Polaxia as fast as this scow could travel. But we had to pass through here. Motherless Eisodos! The Gateway to the Milky Way!"

"You could have gone around," Carpenter observed.

"Right. A privateer running dark and silent, trying to evade the station patrols. They'd have blown our backsides all the way to Betelgeuse. The Wohmagz on Polaxia are the best physicians in the known universe. We thought maybe they could help her..."

Couv broke off and both men shivered as the voices behind them, delicate feminine and guttural masculine, blended together in a climactic cry that ran through the men like lightning through a steel rod.

"She's bleeding over," Couv whispered. Carpenter shuddered and nodded.

After several moments Dram's voice, high and desperate, reached them. "Couv, get the syringe! Quick!"

With preternatural speed Couv spun around, lowered the force field and rammed the syringe he drew from his pocket into the woman's upper arm. She rose snarling, and Carpenter had a fleeting impression of flushed features and huge amethyst eyes.

"They used every purple crayon in the box," he muttered, only half-aware he voiced his chaotic thoughts aloud.

The woman collapsed to the floor. Couv tossed the green coat over her, pulled his brother to his feet and dragged him out of the cell. A grateful Carpenter listened to the force field whooshing back into place. The older Draconier propped Dram against the wall, frowning as his brother slid down it, turned his head and puked. Dram wiped his mouth on his shirt sleeve, grinned up at Couv and the Commander and said, "She's better than chocolate. If she doesn't kill you."

Couv ripped out orders and his crewmen obeyed in a fashion that left Carpenter envious. Carpenter wondered if the medical crew teleported to get there. They froze the woman with a chilling speed.

The three retreated to the Captain's cabin. Once behind the solid bulwark of the oak door they passed the brandy between them in silence, each taking a long unbroken pull.

Carpenter shook his head when the bottle came his way again. "Where in the name of all that's holy did you get this woman?"

"Sss my fault," Dram mumbled. He swayed on his feet and his eyes glazed.

"Dram, go lie down," Couv snapped.

"Mmm all right."

"Dram," Couv spoke like one would to a small child, "I'm the Captain, and I'm giving you an order. Go—lie—down!"

Couv caught his brother as he buckled and with rough hands dumped him onto the bunk. He turned back to Carpenter.

"Please, Commander, if we might be seated."

Carpenter sat, none too certain of his own legs. Ensconced behind the desk, Couv picked up the dagger. He toyed with it, flipping it end over end, catching the hilt each time.

"Have you ever heard of the Caphirate of Olim?" he asked at last.

"That's a myth," Carpenter responded.

Couv gave a harsh laugh. "I dare say your grandfather wished that."

A chill spiraled through Carpenter's middle and radiated outward until his fingers and toes tingled. "What are you saying?"

Couv smiled, part pity, part disbelief. "They never told you, did they? Mother always said they hushed it up. But, I thought maybe they'd at least told you."

"Told me what? What the devil are you talking about?"

"Your grandfather, Jonathan Aster Carpenter, didn't invent the Light Drive. He stole it from the Caphirs."

Carpenter shot to his feet, his fist connecting with Couv Draconier's jaw. "You're a liar!"

Couv's head rocked back, but he shook it off never lifting fist or weapon in retaliation even when Carpenter cocked to strike again. He just sat there, smiling that pity-filled smile.

"The Caphirs raided Earth for centuries taking all the psychics they could catch or carry. The Caphirs are the vampires and abducting aliens of your old Earth tales—they live for the energies they can suck off certain kinds of people. They like empaths best, but telepaths, even just the intuitive will do in a pinch. They latched on to your grandmother. Your granddad found out about them, beat them off, and stole the Light Drive out of one of their ships. He built a fleet to keep the Caphirs off Earth. Then the first delegation from Polaxia arrived. They'd had their own problems with the Caphirs. After that the purges started."

"Purges?" Carpenter sank back in his seat, hoping it would swallow him so he wouldn't have to hear any more.

"Humans are such xenophobes. They hated admitting to the differences among them. They hated the thought of being preyed on by aliens even more. They even hated the Polaxians, but they feared them and what might happen to little, blue Earth if Polaxia allied itself with the Caphirate."

"Get to the purges," Carpenter snapped.

"My grandfather and my mother spoke out against them. So did your grandfather, for what it's worth. Earth decided it had a psychic problem, and that it had to handle that problem expediently. They declared martial law, rounded up and put into camps everybody and anybody believed to have a breath of psychic ability."

"Camps." Carpenter's stomach somersaulted. He remembered the secret books about old Earth's Nazi regime buried in their cellar that he had read at his grandfather's urging.

Couv's inexorable voice continued. "They rammed

through laws about mandatory testing, training and licensing and executed those who protested or refused to cooperate."

"No," Carpenter whispered. "It can't be true. There'd be traces, evidence."

"Oh there are. If you know what to look for and you don't mind running the risk of getting killed. Ordered to do so, the 'loyal' telepaths bent minds and altered memories. You won't find much."

"Oh God."

"Don't feel so bad, Commander. Polaxia, for all its intellect and high moral tone, did little better than Earth. Some Polaxians thought it better to have the Earthen psychics well in hand. Others said Polaxia should not interfere in Earth's problems. Still others feared the Caphirate would look to Polaxia to fill its need with Earth's supply of psychics cut off. My own forbearers retreated to the home world, dragging dear feckless daddy with them."

"This is a nightmare," Carpenter said.

"You have a gift for understatement," Couv mused. From the bunk, Dram cried out from his stupor, as if in pain.

"She's so strong," Couv whispered. "Even the

cryogenic sleep may not hold her much longer. The crew has started having strange dreams. And ever since he found her..." he shook his head towards the bunk, "...Dram's been more and more caught up in thoughts of her. Mother had us tested and registered as children, and we had only the usual bond found between identical twins. Until now. Until Dram slept with her. Sometimes it's like she's eating him alive."

"It's not like that, Couv." Dram's tired voice startled them both. He hung his feet over the side of the bunk. "She's just so scared, and she needs so much..." He looked at Carpenter. "We searched for the Caphirate out of boredom. Mother had been threatening to cut off our money if we didn't come back to Polaxia to take our place in court. I had a map and Couv had a star chart. So we gave Mummy the finger and headed for deep space. To the surprise of all concerned we met the Caphirs. We wined them, dined them, parleyed with them, and at last got an invitation to the home world itself."

Couv stabbed the dagger back into the desktop. "They promised us contracts with the largest, oldest shipping house in the Caphirate. They might have given them to us, too. But Dram just couldn't bring himself to sleep aboard the ship at night."

"I wanted something different," Dram said. "We knew they still kept humans. We'd seen them. Some of the most beautiful men and women you've ever set eyes on, Commander, with every shade of human hair imaginable, and all with these deep, dark amethyst eyes. We figured they'd been breeding them ever since they lost access to Earth."

"A whole race of exquisite, tractable, psychic sponges," Couv said, "just sucking up emotions and experiences and pumping them back out into the Caphirs."

"Not all so tractable," Dram muttered. "Some of those sponges resist. I'd been drinking regular with this sleazy guy in a dive off the spaceport that offered the local hooch and hookers, getting blasted every night and working my way through the girls. One night this jerk offers me a chance at one of the high Caphirate's psychics who'd run away from her master. The jerk and his buddies had caught her on the streets and offered her on a first come, first serve basis, planning on getting everything they could from her until her master found her or she burned out."

Couv shook his head. "Your habits and attitudes are a disgrace to your family and your races, Dram. Both of them."

"Kiss off, Couv. I paid the jerk, and he led me back to this stinking little room. From the moment I touched her, I understood nothing would ever be the same again." Dram's eyes had widened, and Carpenter knew he wasn't seeing the room around him. "She knew what I wanted. I didn't even have to ask. We just wrapped around each other in the bed. Her master kicked in the door. He grabbed her, hurt her. I could feel it down in my bones. I didn't think; I picked up Provocation and ran him through."

"Provocation?" Carpenter blinked and raised his eyebrows.

"The name of the sword." Couv indicated the broadsword that leaned against the wall beside the desk. "A moldering legacy from dear daddy's side of the family."

"There's no mold on that blade." Dram gave his brother a long-suffering look. "A little blood maybe, but no mold." He returned to the subject. "The Caphir master died and all Hell broke loose. I grabbed Dama, decked the guy who'd been selling her in the face, and ran for the ship. The Caphirate's foot solders kicked in the bay door behind me, so I gave orders to liftoff without permission. Couv slid us past their navy by the skin of our teeth, then he opened the engines wide and beat it for home."

"Dama?" Carpenter questioned.

"The woman. She never speaks. In her thoughts she calls herself, 'Taleefah.' It's a Caphirate word for 'sweetmeat.' I won't call her that. I call her 'Dama.' It's Polaxian for 'lady.'"

"You hear her thoughts?"

"Sometimes. Sometimes I just feel what she's feeling." Dram turned his gaze to his brother. "Don't let him kill her, Couv. She hasn't done anything wrong."

"Wait." Carpenter held out his hand. "I have no intention of killing her."

"You have no choice." Couv's frigid voice sent chills down Carpenter's spine. "The laws of Earth, Eisodos and Polaxia state that if an unregistered, untested, unlicensed psychic is discovered, said psychic is to be executed on the spot."

"No way."

"Call your computer if you don't believe me."

Carpenter did. When Eisodos Central confirmed the law he felt the blood drain from his face. His stomach jerked into a knot and acid washed up the back of his throat.

"Tell me, Commander," Couv drawled, "what do you think the current scions of Earth and the many races that pass through Eisodos will do when they learn humans are being held captive and used as fodder for a gutless, life-sucking race? What will they do when they learn there's a law requiring you to execute a helpless woman whose only crime is having been bred to be a mental transmitter? My mother is fond of a saying from your old Earth book, the Bible. It says there's a time to be born and a time to die. Right now it appears that it could be the latter."

Carpenter looked at Drambuie Draconier and noted the hands resting on the grips of his pistols. Dread gripped his heart and soul. "You don't want to do this. It's suicide. Laws can be changed. I will pledge my life for Dama's. Just let my

security chief take her into custody. I'll stay here and help you find a way to free her. I'll see to it all of the resources of Eisodos are turned to the task."

Courvoisier Draconier stood, his right hand falling to the hilt of his katana, his left to the *Om-Gladiv-Zung*. Drambuie rose and stepped to his brother's side, the great sword Provocation appearing in his left hand as if by magic.

"I thank you, Commander Jonathan Aaron Carpenter, for your words. I believe them to be honorable ones. But, I must refuse to give you Dama and to accept your help. Even if I trusted the righteous intentions of human men, had no quarrel with the Caphirate for keeping slaves, and agreed with a law that murders the innocent for being, I still would have to decline your offer."

Carpenter stood as well, dumbfounded. "Why?"

"Because my brother and I have been charged by the *Nana-Naga-Nagagda* of Polaxia themselves: 'As you are *Raxax*, True Knights and Wielders of the Blitzsword, let no hand be laid on the woman known as Taleefah, also called Dama, and let none hinder you in bringing her straightway to the safety of Polaxia and to us. For in her body she bears the child who is the one acknowledged heir to the world, the crown and the throne.' So you see, Commander, I cannot let you leave this ship. And if Dama is injured, confined or in any way prevented from reaching the Nine Immortal, Earth and Polaxia will be at war."

.

The End

About the author: Margreta Eubanks is a long-time member, past president and past newsletter co-editor of the Wichita Area Romance Authors, a chapter of Romance Writers of America. She is a past first place winner of The Emerald City Opener contest by the Seattle RWA Chapter, and she has also judged in several contests

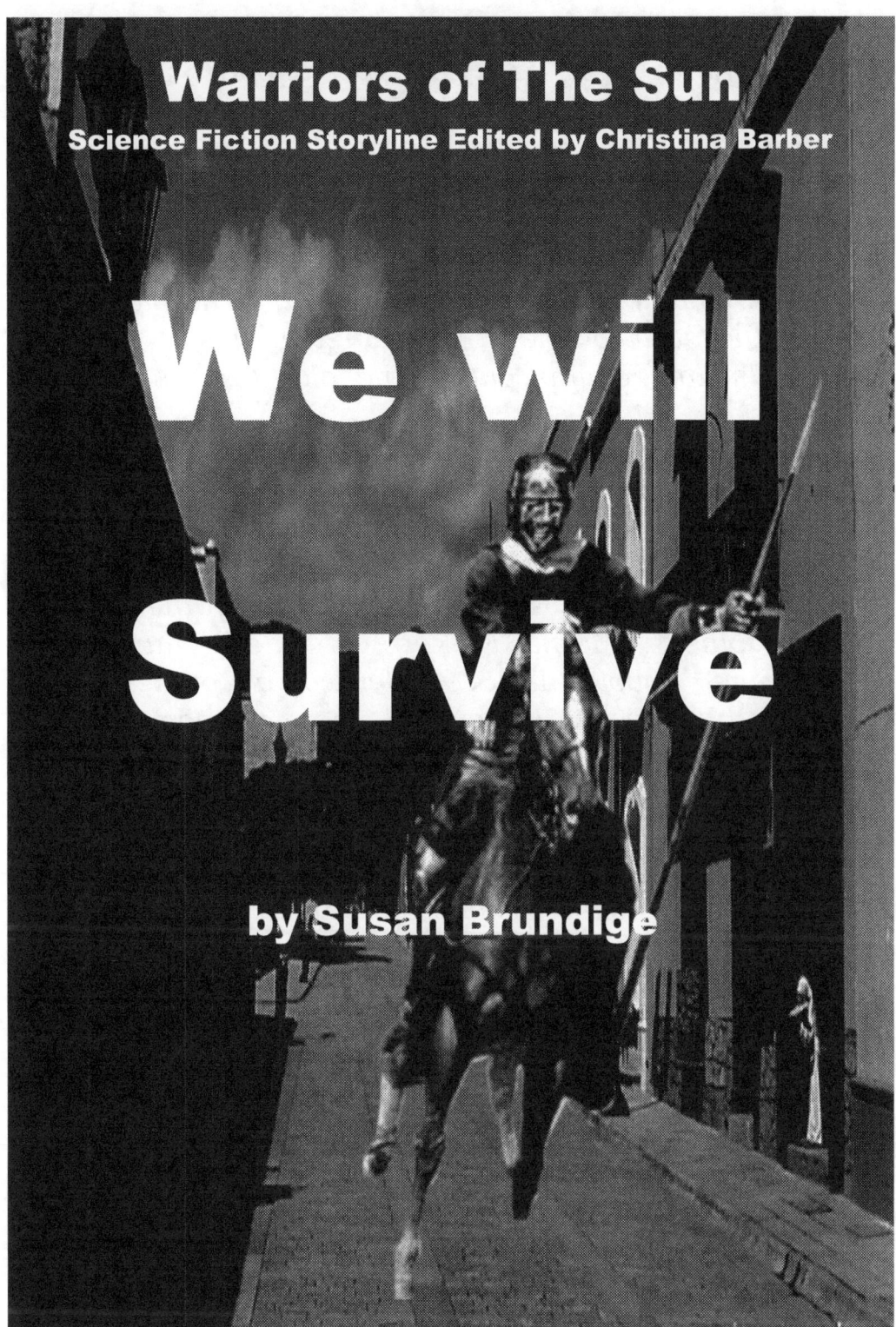

Warriors of The Sun
Science Fiction Storyline Edited by Christina Barber

We will
Survive

by Susan Brundige

Earth is a post-apocalyptic world shattered by a natural disaster. The sun's solar flares went awry, scorching the planet. Sandstorms swirl, carrying pelting sands and the stench of decaying corpses. At night the barren landscape glows an eerie red, occasionally omitting flares of heat. 'The blast' as the survivors term it, created a desert like landscape reminiscent of the old west, ghost town.

Dillion Hollis leads the small group of survivors. Included among the group are: The Crosby family, Terrance, Julie, ten year old Megan, and two month old Joey. Jessica Baldwin, a teen separated from her father in the blast. Marge Parker, an elderly nurse. Tammy Abbot and Scott Jerrico, a couple in their twenties. And Lee Nicholson, a repairman in his fifties.

Zombies and raiders frequently visit the small town, plaguing the survivors. Should they seek others of their kind – if any remain alive - or should they protect what little they have?

Our first story 'We Will Survive' by Susan Brundige brings us into the difficult, daily life of the survivors. In a rough, rugged, unforgiving land where only few can survive.

Christina Barber
Horror Editor

© Susan Brundige

We will Survive

Dillion sat on a wooden chair, in front of what used to be the modern day version of a saloon, swinging doors and all, cleaning the rust from a rifle barrel he'd found. The building's steel frame and fire proof block walls had survived the fires. With some fixing up, they had made the place habitable. It didn't look like much, but they were safe. A mountain of rocks and dirt shaded the building at the back. They had found drinkable water seeping into a small pond below it, though Margie insisted they boil it first. Margie, an RN in her old life, was a life saver. She watched over of the group like a mother hen.

Dillion dampened the corner of a rag with spit, touched the sand and rubbed until the metal shone bright and then he rubbed it with axle grease. He took another rag and with a narrow stick, purged the barrel of debris and greased it too. Covering it carefully with a piece of an old shirt, he laid it where it wouldn't get dirty and began whittling a handle for it.

Only a few healthy people remained as far as he could tell. Those that hadn't reached proper shelter now turned into mindless, flesh eating Zombie like creatures. The small group he lived with was some of the lucky ones. The raiders were just idiots who killed, robbed, and stole for the fun of it. They hadn't changed; they probably did the same before the blast.

Dillion had been in the army before the blast. He'd been a trained specialist and the small group of survivors drew to him as leader. Being a solitary man, he found it hard to live in the midst of such a close group. Yet, he couldn't turn his back on these people or any others who were out there fighting for their lives. "We will survive, because I'll make sure of it." He murmured to himself.

Dillion sighed as he sanded the piece of wood and carefully chipped out the center to fit against the rifle.

"How much more do you have to do, Mr. Hollis?"

"Not much. " He turned the handle this way and that, picked up more sand to smooth the wood so she wouldn't get stuck with splinters.

Megan, who had just turned ten this month, sat on the porch watching carefully as he fitted the pieces together. This rifle was for her and thus, made to fit her small frame.

The air was clear today. There had only been one fire-blast, and that had been a half mile away. The blasts were becoming fewer and Dillion hoped maybe one day they would stop.

Dillion believed time would bring back the plants, if they could find more water. There was a small amount of water beneath the ground and maybe enough water seeped up to grow the few plants they had found. The gas driven vehicles had blown up when the blasts hit. The fuel and transportation was lost. He just hoped to still be here when Earth began to regenerate.

"Now, Megan, have your daddy take you for target practice, but remember, every shot has to count. We don't have a lot of ammo." He

patted the top of her head and sighed once more.

"But he can't see. He lost his glasses." She looked up at him, disappointed.

"Maybe he can see well enough at a distance. If not, we'll practice tomorrow, when I get back." Terrance could see distance, but nothing clearly up close without his glasses. This was tragic to Terrance since he was a botanist.

"Where are you going?"

"To the traders."

"Aren't you afraid?" she asked. Her pretty blue eyes were round with worry.

"Naah, I can run faster and shoot straighter." He teased and grinned. She giggled and ran to show off her weapon. It seemed a crying shame that a child her age should have to carry any kind of weapon, or have to learn to kill to keep safe from harm.

A couple days ago, Terrance and Julie Crosby found some plant life in a small cave when they climbed into the rocks. A mustard plant and a few wild radishes had survived. The wind probably blew the seeds into the rocks where it was damp. They cared for the plants like they were gold. The seeds from those plants would make a big difference in their food supply.

Before the blast, those types of plants were considered a nuisance, growing everywhere, but now, they might prevent starvation. At least it hadn't been nuclear so animal and plant life, if found was clean from contamination.

Jessica Baldwin sat on the building, keeping watch, bored to tears. She shied away from thinking about her father. When they ran for the shelters, she became separated from him. When she thought of him being a zombie it made her sick to her stomach and she wanted to cry. Instead, she thought about other things. Anger was the only thing that took the fear and sorrow away for any amount of time.

She was fifteen for God's sake. She should be going to the sweetheart's ball, playing soccer in school and all the things teens did. But no, here she sat with a rifle in her hands, watching sand dunes and fire balls, praying she never saw another of the zombie people again. The raiders, she could take, though they were dangerous, but the walking dead was freaky. She prayed one of those things wasn't her dad.

Suddenly she squinted. Had something moved out there?

"Dillion!" She called. "I think there is something out there." She lay on her stomach watching. A black thing bobbed on the horizon. She gasped when a huge figure loomed over her.

"Get inside, tell the others. Put up the shutters." Dillion ordered and dropped into place squinting at the horizon.

Jessica scuttled down the ladder and ran for the back door, calling to the others as she ran. "They're coming. Put the shutters up."

She grabbed Joey, the two month old baby and laid him in his bed, made from an empty grenade box. She kissed his chubby cheek and ran for a peep hole, never once letting go of her rifle.

Terrance held the makeshift shutters up while Julie locked them in place. They worked quickly then grabbed their guns.

"Get back there with him Megan. Keep down." Scott said while surveying the front. He put the tip of his rifle in the slot and watched as riders topped the sand dunes and stood looking at the small town.

Jessica moved closer to Marge Parker, who sat at

the table as though nothing bothered her. Jessica knew differently because once in a while she saw her flinch. *Well, I'm scared too* - she thought and patted the older lady's shoulder. "We'll be all right. Dillion and Lee are up top and they shoot pretty good."

Lee climbed the ladder and dropped beside Dillion. Dillion laid out the ammo for Lee and himself.

"I strung wire about neck high, to keep the back of the building safe. If riders tried to go there, they would be thrown off the horse." Lee said, taking his place beside Dillion.

"Good."

Black dots bobbed where the sand met the sky, too far away to make them out, but the dust clouds gave them reason to believe the horses were running toward them at full speed. They weren't carrying a white flag and that meant they weren't friendly.

"You know, Lee, we could use a couple of those horses."

Lee chuckled. "Sure, we'll go right out there and ask for one."

"Smart ass." Dillion laughed quietly. "We could let one of them get close and shoot him out of the saddle."

"Yeah, and who'll grab the horse?"

"Here they come." They both pulled kerchiefs over their nose and mouth. The dust rose, making it hard to pick a target. Mostly the raiders looked like dusty shadows, with their faces painted black and their coats flapping like misshapen wings. Devils came to mind. They had no thought of the future, only now. Killing and stealing was their thing.

Dillion snorted. The idiots probably saw some old vampire movie and decided it would scare them. Well, this was no movie, it was stark reality and the worst nightmare he could have thought up didn't compare.

With the rifle on his shoulder and the hot sun beating down upon them, he counted an even dozen as they raced for the saloon, bullets flying everywhere. A bullet hit the wood, sending splinters at his face. Dillion waited until one of the raiders came nearly to the porch and shot him out of the saddle. The man flew backwards off the horse and landed in the dust. He didn't move.

Lee's shot took the top of a man's head. "Got you, you rat." He muttered.

Below, more shots took two more down and wounded another.

Five of the riders were down. One scrambled to his feet and ran after the others. He grabbed at the bridles of a loose horse, mounted and rode away.

Dillion kept a sharp eye out as the horse ran to the back of the building, right where Dillion hoped he'd go. He hurried down the ladder and ran around the building. He nearly whooped with joy. The horse drank from the bucket of water he put there earlier, hoping this would happen.

"Hey boy, ahh, girl." He said after a glance down, then gently took hold of the reins and removed the makeshift saddle and tied the reins to the back porch post. This horse was a God send.

He hadn't told the others about his plan to go farther out to hunt for more survivors. The horse would help him cover more ground.

"Dillion, Jessica was hit." Lee yelled from inside.

Leaving the horse, Dillion ran, skidded to a stop at the door jam, gripping it hard, afraid of what he'd see.

Jessica sat glaring at Lee. "I told you I was fine."

Relief hit him so hard, he felt lightheaded. He never had children and always thought one day he would get married and have a house full. There didn't seem any chance of that now. These children were the only hope for the future and had to be protected at all cost if they had any chance of rebuilding.

She lifted her chin and grinned at Dillion. "I have my first scar. Kind'a like a Tattoo."

Marge smeared salve on the shallow cut. "I'd say more like a permanent part."

Dillion squatted in front of Jessica. "Take it easy on the tattoos. You'll get more than your share before you have a chance to grow up. Leave the fighting to the men and help protect the little ones."

Jessica gave an exaggerated sigh. "Okay, but I got one at least." She laughed. "Did you see that idiot land in the sand? He got up and ran like his butt was on fire." They laughed, relieved that they had all come through the battle in one piece.

Lee and Scott started the repairs to the building. It was sturdy, but the wood still had the smell of smoke, though it had only been scorched. They had lined the inside of the wooden part of the building with what ever metal they could find, mostly scraps of metal from abandoned cars and other vehicles.

The women wiped the dust from the furniture and proceeded with getting supper. Dillion took Megan and Jessica out to see the horse. Its coloring might be that of a Pinto, but more black than anything, with a white nose. The raiders must have taken good care of the animal because he had no fear of them.

"It's big." Megan said, hanging back.

"Ohhh." Jessica said and went right up to the horse. It snuffled her fingers, making her giggle.

Megan eased closer and put her hand out. When the horse snuffled her hand, she yipped, and then reached out again.

"She's soft." Megan petted her neck and crooned to her. The horse ate up the attention.

Dillion had plans for the horse. "What are we going to feed the horse?"

"I found grass between the rocks." Jessica said.

"I know, honey, but I've been waiting for it to spread. It's thick and spreads by the roots. If we let her at it, she'll destroy the roots. We

need to get plant life started again."

"I know. Are you going to the traders tonight?"

He nodded. "We need food. What we have won't last long."

Dusk turned the sky dark with red streaks. Dillion wished for clouds. A good rain would bring out more plant life, but there wasn't a cloud in the sky. There hadn't been a single cloud in the sky for weeks and without rivers and the ocean, there wouldn't be. He found an old piece of sheet metal and tied a rope to it. He wanted to build a rock fence in front of their shelter. It wouldn't stop the raiders, but it might slow them down. At least keep them from getting too close to the building.

Dillion left on foot that night, wearing dark rags to cover his body and head. The pack he carried was heavy with chunks of metal fittings and other useful things, such as an old oil lamp and iron skillet. It wouldn't buy much, but anything was better than nothing.

He ran at a steady trot, staying clear of the open areas. The stench hit him before he caught sight of a pack of zombies devouring one of their own. The smell nearly gagged him. One could never get used to the smell of rotting flesh. They had been the unlucky ones. Feeling sorry for them was useless. They had no viable thoughts. They were flesh eaters, nothing more. Before he'd met up with his group, he'd found people who knew they were turning. They killed themselves rather than be like the others. He would have done the same. He didn't understand why they didn't just die. How could they live when their brains were nothing but deteriorated mush? Soon they would be gone, taking one more worry with them into oblivion.

He dropped to the ground and crab walked, keeping as low as he could, skirting the pack, but never taking his eyes off them. Once he felt safe, he jumped to his feet and ran like hell. He needed to get back before daylight. The trader only worked nights. Dillion came upon them by accident before he found his small group. He didn't ask where they got the supplies because it didn't matter. They had them and he needed them.

Sweat covered his body by the time he reached the trader. It looked like an old eighteen hundreds dugout, only it had a steel door and guards. He uncovered his head and the guard let him through. Sacks of dry goods sat along one wall and cinnamon scented the air. Shelves filled with tools and bits and pieces of stuff that had been brought in to trade for food. The candle light was so dim Dillion could hardly see.

"Hey, Dillion." A balding heavyset man, wearing overalls and a worn t-shirt, called from behind a wooden barrel table. "What'cha got for me tonight?"

Dillion laid out his bits and pieces on the barrel. "I need flour and rice."

The man pursed his lips and gave the pile of silverware and one Corning ware bowl in remarkably perfect shape, a skeptical look. "I can give you a twenty-five pound bag of flour, but it's not enough for rice."

Dillion brought out the iron skillet and saw the man's eyes widen. He had scoured and seasoned it before bringing it.

"That, my friend will get you the rice."

Then Dillion set the oil lamp on the barrel. "I need a pair of glasses, powdered milk, salt and baking powder."

The man picked up the lamp and skillet and set them behind him, grinning.

"You got it and then some. Pick out what you need, my man."

"The glasses?" Dillion asked, hopeful.

The big fellow grinned and snatched a wooden case from a shelf behind him, laid it on the counter, unsnapped the lock and pulled the lid back. Neat little rows of glasses lay in the black velvet. Since Terrance was far sighted Dillion had to make sure it to get the right ones. Finally he picked up a pair and wrapped it, opened the twenty pound bag of rice and shoved it down deep inside.

Dillion, taking advantage of the man's generous mood, picked up a small bag of grainy looking seeds. "What's this?"

"I don't know. Toss it in with your stuff." The man glanced at the door. "It's coming on close to midnight. You'd better be going."

"Have you seen other survivors?" Dillion asked.

"That's how I keep going. Now, if you want to know if I know where any are located, no, I don't. No one wants to give out their locations because of the raiders."

"Thanks." Dillion covered his head, loaded his bag and slung it over his shoulder. He nodded at the man and slid out the door. He ran for a couple miles, before setting the bag down to even the load. Straps were sewn unto it and now he put them over his shoulders.

Suddenly a noise caught his attention and he crouched. What had he heard?

Yip, yip, yip. He eased around the rock and found a mother dog, nursing a puppy. She growled at him, but her tail wagged. A Beagle. *How in heck had she survived out here?* He wondered.

"Hello girl." He scratched her ears. She was weak and looked starved. The puppy practically sucked all the life out the mother dog and she would let it because she didn't know any better.

He took off his coat, wrapped her in it and tied the arms around his neck and stuck the pup under his arm. He traveled at a fast trot, by-passing the area where the zombies were last seen and sighed with relief when he saw the saloon.

Trust was a rare commodity these days. The trader might send his men out to take back what he'd given out. So Dillion made sure to leave no tracks and went a different way back to camp each time. The fact that others came to trade gave him hope. If they could find others like themselves, they could start rebuilding. Strength in numbers.

Lee came out to meet him. He took the bag from Dillion and slung it over his shoulder and they went inside. "You look worn out."

Dillion sat the dog on the floor, put the puppy beside her. He threw off the rags covering his body and hung them on a nail. "Brought something for the kids."

Marge knelt to care for the dog. "She's half starved."

Dillion grinned, knowing Marge would fix her up. "The zombies were out in force tonight. Now they've begun fighting each other."

Lee shuddered. "Nasty bunch. Hope I never meet one again."

Dillion nodded. "They won't last much longer."

"I feel kind of sorry for them. It's not their fault they are that way." Lee said.

"I know."

Marge came to the table. "What have we here?"

"I got what I could. He took out the bag of seeds from his pocket. "I'm not sure what this is, but Terrance might."

Marge turned to the supplies. Since it was nearly time for breakfast, she mixed

up a pan of biscuits and made gravy. She wondered how Dillion carried that huge pack on his back. Then to pick up a dog and its pup seemed unreal. Almost everything he did was beyond any of the other men's endurance. He was the kind of man she would have wanted for her daughter.

Thinking of her daughter brought tears to her eyes. She'd lost both her daughter and grandson. She'd give anything to see them again.

Elkina and Erick. Elkina had studied to be a doctor and been an intern when the blast hit. Now, she didn't know if they were alive or not. Erick was every bit as bright as his mother and so loving. Tears ran down her cheeks and she felt angry at herself for not having the courage to look for them, she swiped them away.

Dillion dug his hand into the rice and brought out the rag covered glasses and handed them to Terrance.

"What's this?" Terrance asked, reaching for them.

"Look and see." Dillion said and crossed his arms, praying they were right for the man.

Terrance eyes widened when he unwrapped the

glasses. He tried them on and read the label on the flour and laughed.

"Oh my God. I can see. They're a little weak, but hell, I can see." He grabbed Dillion and slapped him on the back. "I'll be forever grateful, man."

Dillion shook the man's hand. "We need you. Can't have you wandering around half blind out there."

"Come get it." Marge called, filling a bowl for the dog. "We'll have to let the kids give you a name." She crooned to the dog as it swallowed a biscuit whole.

Julie grabbed his arm to stop him. "Thank you Dillion. He felt useless."

"We need every man, woman and child, Julie. I might be gone at times, looking for others like us and he'll have to be in top shape."

"There has to be more. If we survived, other might." She said, leading the way to the table.

"I'd like to start digging into the side of the mountain tomorrow. We need a place for the women and children to go and to hide our supplies if we're attacked by a big party."

"I think there might be a cave. When Tammy and I were back there, the ground caved in. We were attacked before we could check it out." Scott said, around a mouthful of biscuit.

"Jessica can keep watch while I get a couple hours sleep. You and Lee dig around up there."

Dillion grabbed a biscuit and headed for his bed.

Julie spent the morning sorting out the seeds. The mixture seemed to be garden seed mixed with bird seed. All of which would come in handy. Any plant life would help bring moisture to the land.

Scott and Terrance spent the morning digging. They found a couple of seedling trees growing beneath the ground and a seeping water pipe.

Terrance, careful not to harm the roots, dug them up and wrapped the root balls in his shirt. The pipe had been smashed by falling rocks and debris. The framing protecting the pipes had burned and the earth collapsed. If he wasn't mistaken, it might mean there should be a tunnel. If they were very lucky, it may still be intact. He didn't want to disrupt the small dribble because that was their only source of water.

Lee moved the rocks aside. "I think the pipe leads back a ways."

"We need shovels."

"We need a lot of things, but from the looks of it, we won't be getting them anytime soon." Lee agreed.

After they'd dug for an hour, Lee stopped and wiped his face with his sleeve. They had piled everything viable to the side. "There are a couple pieces of steel big enough to grind into shovels and plenty of loose wood for the handle."

"If we can make decent tools, Dillion can trade them at the traders." Lee said, picking up a fist sized rook and began shaping the metal into shovels

Meantime, Scott and Terrance built a rock shelter for the horse. They carried rocks from the back and piled them in an A shape fence to keep it from falling. It was high enough to discourage the horse from straying.

That night Dillion planned to go out further. He threw on the pathetic excuse for a saddle on the horse and rode north. The only safe time for traveling was at night. He had a bag filled with things for the trader, but first he wanted to look around. He'd ridden close to three miles when he saw a flicker of light, then it was

gone. He dismounted and walked in that direction. After a few minutes, he gave up and headed for the trader. The shovels Lee made might get them extra supplies. He hoped. That night he exchanged the tools and scraps for food supplies and a bag of ammo. Most important was finding out where that light came from.

He criss-crossed the area until him and the horse were worn out. Finally he gave up and headed home. Tomorrow night, he planned to ride closer to the mountains, but hoped he didn't run into raiders or zombies.

Dillion walked the horse, leaning low to hunt the ground for any sign of tracks. Just as he sat straight, he caught sight of the light again. This time he followed it. He climbed up into the saddle and rode toward the small glow.

Concentrating on the light, he failed to see the two men in black, right in front of him. They jumped up at him, grabbing at the horse. Dillion kicked one in the head with his foot and grabbed the other by the hair. His horse bucked and turned in circles while the man he held screamed in pain. Finally, tired of the fool, he slammed his fist into the man's nose and dropped him. The other was out cold when Dillion dismounted and rolled him over. They were young, maybe just out of their teens. They carried knives and pistols in their belts. He took all the weapons and any ammo he could find and left them lying where they fell. In the daylight, he would have eliminated them so they wouldn't be a threat, but just maybe one or two might come looking for shelter and he couldn't bring himself to do it.

Dillion took the reins of his horse and walked a little ways. From the ground, Dillion couldn't see the light, so he mounted and began following it once more. When he came close, he tied the horse to an outcropping of rocks and went in by foot. A dark figure loomed up beside him and without thinking

Dillion bashed the man over the head with his gun and jumped at the tent. The flap hit his face as he landed on hands and knees inside.

"Don't move, mister or I'll blow your head off." A very feminine voice ordered.

"I'm friendly," he said and put his hands in the air and sat up. "Turn the light out. There are raiders looking for you. I came up against two sneaking in on you."

A boy, maybe ten, threw dirt over the small fire. Before the light dimmed, Dillion saw three small girls and the woman. Inside he laughed. They were exactly what he hoped to find. Since these people were alive maybe there were more healthy people who needed to be found. Then his eyes met the woman's golden gaze and he could only stare.

Life was looking up.

The End

About the author: Susan Brundige loves to write westerns and was thrilled to work on a futuristic type western. She has five children, four grandchildren and one on the way. This is her first short story acceptance and she is very pleased to have sold her story to us. Life is good.

To Save Pearl
Time Travel Storyline Edited by Darlene Oakley

Kaden's

Incentive

By

Jennifer DiCamillo

Dear Readers,

Marshall Kaden has always been fascinated by time travel, to visit times that he'd only ever read about in books, to see people who, for some reason or other, became legends. In our first installment Kaden decides to revisit the events surrounding the Japanese attack on Pearl Harbor that results in over 1500 deaths of sailors, servicemen, soldiers, nurses, doctors, pilots....It is the attack that brought the United States into World War II in the Pacific and into the conflict across the Atlantic.

"What if" theories abound about what happened, how the whole tragedy could have been prevented and what would have happened to the people, the U.S., the world at such a pivotal moment of history. The changes could be effective or not. One never knows with time travel.

Also uncertain and elusive is how exactly one travels to the past. This was the challenge to our writers--write a story with technology, theory and conflicting non-interference rules.

Jennifer DiCamillo's story, "Kaden's Incentive", is an imaginative twist to this storyline taking us into the heart of the American government, the White House, and the office of President Roosevelt. We meet not only the President, but the legendary First Lady. Pulp fiction allows for freedom of expression and imagination and I feel Jennifer has done that in this story.

Darlene Oakley
Time Travel Editor

© Jennifer DiCamillo

Kaden's Incentive

"**O**kay, now remember, stick to your orders or you could screw up our very existence. Earth could be destroyed or renewed depending on what you do. Messing with history is tricky."

Shrugging into his specially lined, leather bomber jacket—a knockoff of the fighter pilot uniform of the U.S. military, circa 1940, Marshall Kaden listened to his instructor, a droid female named Sixta. A battle-axe robot, some called her—behind her back, she was the only female in residence at EBDO-7, Earth Bio-Dome Outpost 7.

Built like an auburn-haired bombshell, cum-fully-stacked sexpot, she was wholly operational overruling any rational thought whenever he was in her presence—even though he knew this condition threatened his very existence. Sixta's green laser eyes could, quite literally, melt you down if you blundered in her vicinity. She sported other, less predictable tricks on occasion, but, for the most part, little miss Sixta was all business with none of the play her appearance promised. He didn't know why she wore mini-skirts and cropped, form-fitting tops, except to perhaps torment the team of scientists she lorded over. At the moment, he noted she had donned hot pink with silver accents, including thigh high stiletto-heeled boots. Her lips shone bright with matching silver lipstick. Only a droid would walk around like that.

But, what a droid.

"Are you listening to me? I can give you a lobotomy, Kaden, if you—"

"Baby, I'm gonna do this dance with a two-step and a triple flip because I know you're gonna come through with a super reward. I am way overdue."

Too cocky, maybe, considering he didn't even know what the job was yet, but it couldn't be anything big. No. Something big might blow up the planet and then where would they be? She wouldn't give him a job *that* important.She spared him a little smile and tipped her head, shooting his schmoozy tone right back at him. "Baby, you are overdue for something, but I'm thinking it's a spanking."

Her rapping of his objective log scroll (OLS) upon her thigh, reminded Kaden that she knew how to give it to him making it difficult for him to pay attention as she outlined his orders.

"Remember the rules. Keep a low profile. Eat and imbibe nothing. Touch as little as possible. Absolutely no sexual contact. Leave no evidence, no information. Give no warnings. Take no souvenirs."

"Cut to the chase, baby. I got the time, the place. I know how I'm gettin' there. What's the job? I got somethin' to do when I get back. No more wasting echo-seconds, all right? You tell me, then you go, get naked in my chamber, and I'll be right back."

"Just do it right, genius."

Marshall thought the IC (Interspatial Command) had all drunk from the murky water basin on the moon they were stationed at on the other side of the galaxy. Messing with history? It was not his idea of a smart move. There were way too many calculations proving probability of error stacking—DE, the domino effect—and, despite several incidents, IC didn't quite get the concept that altering previa could bleep them out of existence.

"If you do this right," Sixta smiled fully for the first time that morning, "You might just get a taste of honey."

The food of the gods. The only thing that didn't spoil. Sounded good. One of the few things that had survived the world wreckage. Gotta love those genetically altered bees. He checked his cache of vitamin enriched honey straws, and purified beverage pouches in pockets inside the right side of his jacket.

The rhythm of the OLS hitting her thigh changed and he frowned.

"I know you can do this, but there are some extenuating circumstances that make this tricky. Just be careful. Okay?"

His arrogance faltered, but he shook off the possibility of failure. "Whatever it is, I'm sure I can handle it." Marshall's lip curled up in a lopsided grin. "Challenge is my middle name." Sounded much better than Bolfoy, the name of his home planet, which was tattooed on his butt in navy blue block letters, as dictated the identification protocols of 2267. In any case, failure was not part of his resume and never would be, if he had anything to say about it.

Sixta's eyebrows peaked, demonstrating for him the amazing collection of technology standing in front of him. So real. He wondered where the original human model was.

He huffed, tapping his foot. "Come on. Just spill the deal."

"You have everything you need in your coat," Sixta said, belaying the announcement further.

Marshall checked the special op facilitators in the left lining of his jacket. There were several toys and tools there. His favorite was the ink pen. The handy little thing let him write anything he wanted and the ink disappeared in about an hour. Rounding out his armoury were: pellet bombs, two portal opening capsules (IDPP), the standard issue tracking iode, which he swallowed; grenade coins, bullet-sized grapler gun, plexi chisel, hook and pick kit; listening and remote viewing devices, night scope, and Photog-L, a pin for visual dimension-linking; and, last but not least, explosive gum. Another one of his favorites.

"Hey! This is great!" The gum wrapper resembled the 1941 Uncle Sam's National Defense pack.

Sixta rolled her eyes. "Put that away. And put your PLP on the lapel. It's a replica of a commendation of the time."

He did as he was told. "This is the one that says I'm an ace, right?"

"Yes. Try to avoid proving that, though, would you? Your Simulator Exercise Numbers are a little weak."

Weak. Ha! He had scored well above average.

As if reading his mind she added, "Above average, but not perfect means you've got too large a margin for error. If you were to, say, take a plane up and get shot down, we'd have to send another operative to find you and bring your sorry dead ass back. So, keep your mitts off the planes."

Real planes. He couldn't wait.

"I think I'm ready to go." He looked up expectantly, his hand out.

She waited a second before slapping the OLS into it. "It's been nice knowing you, Kaden."

He opened it and blinked. Then blinked again.

Prevent deforestation devastation by impressing the President of the U.S. of forestry preservation importance, and prevent Pearl Harbor Attack.

Preserving the planet was one thing, but prevent Pearl Harbor?

"Authentic papers of identification and recommendation for duty will be in the hands of a man coming toward you after you *portal-in*. No one else should be there, if we've calculated properly. All you have to do is snag his paperwork and roll him into the portal. The rest will become apparent when you see what he's carrying."

Sixta pushed his outgoing Inter-Dimensional Portal Pill (IDPP), pre-set with the date and place the IC thought most likely to do his trick, into his mouth. "Like I said, nice knowing you. Now, bite and spit."

He rolled it in his mouth a minute, sliding it around with his tongue. He did *not* want to do this. Prevent Pearl Harbor? What the hell were they thinking?

"Spit! That's an order."

Marshall cracked the pill with his teeth then turned and spat on the floor. Catalyzed by his saliva, the IDPP grew until, a few echo-

secs later, it was large enough to step through.

He had perfected the Inter-Dimensional Portal Pill (IDPP), himself, motivated by having once witnessed a portal open only half way and an operative blipped into lala land when it closed on him as tried to squeeze through.

His brilliance was a lazy, self-motivated thing. He created masterpieces of small technology that worked for him and simplified his life in the freaking, falling-apart bio-dome on the now nearly abandoned Earth. If it had been up to him, he would have scrapped the planet, made it the universal dumpsite, and moved on.

Grinning, he said, "Get naked, baby."

With that, he stepped through the portal. Dimensions slipped wormhole style and his vision skewed, as the world around him stretched into prismatic color, and then, he was there. In another time and place.

It took him a minute to get his bearings. He'd somehow expected to be put on the beach in Hawaii, but no, he was, apparently, in an old musty building...alone. He frowned. He was supposed to contact the President of the United States. How in hell was he going to do that? Where the hell was he? And where was the man he was supposed to roll into the portal? He only had a few more seconds before it closed.

Nanos passed. His heart beat faster. Just like IC to screw something like this up. The portal collapsed with no man and Kaden knew the mission was doomed.

With the one portal closed he'd have to use one of his IDPP's when the man came. Muttering a few expletives, he put one in his mouth and rolled it around.

Click. Click. Click. A woman turned the far corner and tapped toward him in sensible black shoes. He was no fashion expert, but no one could call those, or her clothing, attractive. Gray service wear. She had a cute face, though, and her body was plumply attractive, curvy, and soft. But, more importantly, she carried papers.

The woman blinked when she saw him. "Major Kaden. Weren't you just..." she glanced over her shoulder, in the direction she'd come.

She knew his name? His heart stopped. What kind of joke had IC played on him this time?

Whatever the mix up he had to play through the scene.

Charm. That usually worked for him.

"Baby, I was just thinking about you." He moved toward her.

She blinked, twisting at the waist, pointing. "But, didn't you just say—"

Marshall put one hand on her papers, the other around her back and smiled down at her. It didn't take an IQ as high as his to figure out that he'd been selected for "double duty." So, there was another man that looked just like him, or enough like him for them to be mistaken for one another—with the same name, no less. Could he be within touching distance of an ancestor of his? This was too weird. Why didn't Sixta warn him?

"I say a lot of things when there's an audience. I got an image to uphold."

"But how did you—?"

He pushed the IDPP into his cheek. "I'm an ace, baby. I'm amazing, or hadn't you heard?"

She smiled.

Marshall tried to keep the antsy feeling from overwhelming him. The mission was already going wrong. Maybe he should bite, spit, and go home, and tell IC to reconfigure.

Abort, his mind said. Abort now! But, this little

secretary was cozying up, and she didn't have a bat or hidden weapons of the ilk Sixta sported. His curiosity had his libido kicking in.

He glanced at the papers. She put them to her chest, despite the fact that he'd fingertipped the top edge, forcing him to let go.

"Don't you have a meeting with the President?"

The President?

"Mr. Roosevelt doesn't like to be kept waiting."

"Ah. Yes. Are you going in to see him?"

"Oh, no. I'm just delivering these orders to his secretary."

"I can take them."

"Uh, I don't think so." She squinted up at him. "You look diff—"

He needed to do something before she realized he wasn't the Major she thought he was. He bit into his IDPP and spat. She stepped back, about to scream when it began to grow. He grabbed her, clamping one hand over her mouth, and pushed her in, ripping the papers from her hand as she fell into the portal.

There was a moment of stunned surprise, slow motion falling, where his gaze met hers, but then she was gone. Then he heard footsteps around the corner. He turned,

struggling with the fear of being discovered with the portal still open. What would he have to do next?

The footsteps were accompanied by a strong whistling tune that Kaden didn't know. The man who appeared had an air of confidence and happiness—who wouldn't be when called to visit the President of the United States?

In an instant, the man saw the portal, Kaden, and the secretary's shoes as her body disappeared. He hunkered down, dropping his papers and charged Marshall, taking him to the floor.

This was not the plan!

The two men wrestled, echo-secs passing as the portal shimmied towards certain collapse. Marshall knew he could be in real trouble. His assailant rolled him to his back and cocked his right hand, but the punch never came, as both men froze, and frowned, at the mirror image of themselves.

The fist dropped. "Who the hell are you?"

"A dead ringer."

They had to be related! Damn IC and Sixta and all the futuristic advancements. There was no way this was a coincidence.

"Wha—?"

"Tell ya about it later." Marshall pushed with all he had, flipping the Major into the portal.

"Deal with that, Sixta."

He knew the man would come up fighting, after landing atop the lovely little lady who'd preceded him. Kaden had changed things already. That woman wasn't going to get her paperwork delivered.

The portal disappeared and Kaden scrambled to pick up the secretary's papers and soldier's orders scattered across the floor. Just as he got to the last piece someone else rounded the corner. He snapped to his feet, tucked the papers inside his coat, then tugged on the waistband of his slacks and straightened his shirt.

What next?

The woman who approached him now wore nothing military, just a simple long wool skirt and cotton blouse.

She wasn't exceptionally pretty even when she greeted him with a brief nod. Her under-pronounced chin drew great attention to her bucked teeth, but she had notable piercing blue eyes.

Her rich alto voice soothed his agitated nerves as she acknowledged him with a duck of her head, "Major."

He fell into step beside her as she headed toward the Presidential chamber, trying to settle his mind about her.

"You are here to see my husband, yes?" She spoke conversationally, as if she were as comfortable with him, a stranger, as anybody she'd known for years. He wondered if she knew the man he'd just dumped into the future.

"Um, yes."

"You have your orders already?"

"I, um—" He pulled them out, waved them around, and then perused them. "Yes. I'm shipping out to Hawaii, looks like."

"I think we're putting all our eggs in one basket, there. I've told Franklin so." Her glance landed on the pin on his lapel.

"You're a pilot?"

"Uh, yes. Yes, I am." For the first time in his life, he felt stupid. Although he had a degree in Old Earth History, he had never expected to walk in the halls of the famed White House, or to find himself in the presence of Eleanor Roosevelt.

"I love flying. Amelia was going to give me lessons." Her lips soured. "But *he* talked me out of it."

He. Franklin. Her husband. The President.

Her second of sadness got to him. Kaden almost offered to take her up in the air, but Sixta's warning rang in his brain.

Amelia...flying... If he was there to prevent the Pearl Harbor attack, he had to be in the year...what? 1941? His mind trailed quickly through the mini-files of his brain. That would mean Amelia...

"Earhart?"

"Yes, but it's too late, you know."

He remembered that Amelia Earhart had disappeared in 1937. "I'm sorry."

"Oh." Her stride faltered. "You know, there are many things that happen that I don't understand."

What could he say to that? I could explain a lot to you, if I had time? He patted his chest where his last IDPP remained. Oh, the things he could tell the First Lady of the United States. She seemed rather lonely, almost terse. What would she be like if she got excited? If she knew secrets the world couldn't even guess at now? Marshall reached up and scratched the back of his head.

"I think we can all say that."

She picked up the pace and they turned the next corner together.

"There are commonalities between all men and women, Major. We just have to look for them."

"Yes. I suppose you're right."

She grinned. "Of course I'm right. I'm the President's wife. Here we are." Two guards stood outside the door.

She asked, "Is he alone?"

The guard on the right stared the Major up and down and Kaden thought he was about to be searched. That would throw a terrible glitch in the annals of history if all his little spy tools became common knowledge before they were even invented. He thought about turning around, leaving her there at the door, but the papers in his hand said to report to the President directly. He was glad he'd looked at them and that fate had brought him to the First Lady's side.

"Yes, ma'am, but..." The guard eyed Kaden suspiciously, "...he's given orders not to be disturbed."

The other checked a timepiece. "He has an appointment in five minutes."

"Well, posh, then. He has five minutes for me. And, I suspect, the Major here is his appointment. Open those doors, please."

The distrustful guard stepped in front of the door. "We'll have to search him."

Eleanor said, annoyed, "Do you think a man would get on the grounds and through the security teams—all the way to this office—if he hadn't already been searched four times? I think you'll just keep your hands to yourself and do as you're told or I'll have you peeling potatoes for dinner."

With that, they gained a coded knock and entry into the Presidential Office, and Kaden had to admire the woman. She lifted her chin as she stepped in with a keening, "Franklin!"

His head swiveled from the window the minute she spoke. "Eleanor!"

"I've brought your Major, early."

"I see that." From his wheelchair, Franklin Delano Roosevelt eyed Marshall with an astute expectation as the door shut discreetly behind them. "You're the flyboy that everybody's patting on the back, eh?"

Kaden shrugged. What else could he do? His stomach turned over on itself. He was standing in FDR's office! Marshall noted that the Oval Office was just as historical accounts had described.

Astounding! "I, uh, can manage all right, I guess."

"You sound like a plowboy." FDR grinned. "I like 'em honest, don't you, Eleanor?"

"Yes," she said, eyeing Marshall with the intensity of Sixta's laser beam. Her perusal made him more nervous than actually standing in front of the President. Curtly, she turned her attention to her husband. "I've come to remind you that Harry Hopkins is meeting you for lunch tomorrow."

"I haven't forgotten. He's my best friend." He rolled his chair toward the large "authentic wood" desk. The piece absolutely shocked Marshall. As he glanced around, he noticed the windows, doors and furniture all accented with wood. What a waste of forest resources. Did they have any idea what cutting down all the trees had done to Earth? He guessed not.

As Franklin wheeled himself into place behind the desk, he landed a heavy hand on it and asked, "A man doesn't forget his best friend, does he, boy?"

Kaden jumped. "No, Sir. Of course not."

"You have one, don't you?"

There was a serious scrutiny. The President narrowed his gaze, and Kaden was forced to think about his relationships. He had none, really, except with Sixta. He told her pretty much everything. Everything he was willing to tell anybody.

He had to. If he didn't, she'd lobotomize him and run cerebral scans over the extracted tissue. And his colleagues? All loners like him, introspective types, paranoid of idea thieves. No, he didn't have any real friends.

The President was waiting for an answer, though, and he had to admit, "Well, Sir. I'm a soldier with very little fortune," implying that all his friends had died, and that wasn't entirely untrue. His friends were those he found in history and scientific manual chips.

FDR's expression darkened and he nodded. "Have a seat, son."

The President rolled his chair around the desk, toward the seating area of sofas, and commanded, "Eleanor, sit. I'm sure you'll enjoy talking to this pilot."

"You think I didn't know what he was?" She sounded almost grouchy as she passed Kaden and sat down in a chair. "You can spot his bomber jacket clear up the hall and the pin is a dead giveaway."

Marshall took a seat when FDR waved with a frown.

"Don't give me that. You can smell the air on him."

"Oh." She smiled and ducked her head. "You're a fool, Franklin. Quit teasing me." She reached down beside her chair and pulled a knitting project out of a wooden box.

Kaden watched Eleanor for a moment as she focused on her needles.

Franklin slapped his own knee and said, "Well, you've probably figured out that we've got some things cooking."

Marshall's eyebrows rose. Cooking? That was the understatement of a lifetime. The President had no idea that the chicken that he had brought to every American's pot had turned into a goose about to be cooked. "Well, Sir. The United States of America has always had an iron in the fire, hasn't it?"

Nervousness assailed him. Something important was about to happen and he was a pivotal factor.

"Yes, it has."

Silence stretched for several seconds and Kaden comprehended that time was longer here, with nothing measured in nanos or echoes. A clock on the wall ticked in heavy, torturous clicks.

"Oh, just get to it, Franklin. You're making the boy sweat."

Boy? He hadn't been called that in a long time. Thirty wasn't that young. But, he took it without offense.

When Franklin clucked his tongue, Marshall realized his mind had wandered a bit. He knew the presidential couple was watching him. He was almost giddy from seeing so much wood in person, from being with such a pivotal couple in history. His fingers itched to touch the polished surface of the table beside his chair.

"Were you picturing yourself somewhere else?" The President didn't give him time to answer before adding, "I do that. Anywhere but in this chair."

That forced Kaden to look at the contraption, which, up until then, he had been avoiding. "I expect adventures of the mind are the best you can do."

"You're right about that!"

In Marshall's time they had neuro-stimulator implants that could repair his legs. How easy it would be for him to grant the President's

wish. But, then, what would he tell people about how he'd been healed? Would they think him insane once word got out that he was healed by traveling to the future. Wouldn't that be worse for the President, the World, the War?

"It's not so bad, most days. But, that's not why you're here."

Kaden marshaled his thoughts back to his orders-- to refocus the President on forestation projects and stop Pearl Harbor. He was still trying to figure out how to achieve the latter.

Really all he had to do was wheedle an invitation to lunch tomorrow, drop a few pointed comments and, when Secretary of War, Henry Stimson called, convince the President that the threat to Pearl was real, and quash any negations Harry Hopkins might put forward. Easy as...pie.

His mouth watered. What did that taste like? There was probably a pie to be had here, with real berries or fruit. He could only imagine! But, Sixta's rules echoed through his brain. Eat and imbibe nothing. He sighed.

Again, FDR grabbed his attention with a slap and rub of thigh, drawing Kaden's gaze to it. "I've got a message for you to deliver. Special delivery, you might say."

Marshall squared his shoulders. Could this be what IC had in mind? Something to do with this message? A delivery from the President of the United States himself?

"Strictly confidential, of course."

They were interrupted by a courier who gained entry with a quick knock from the security team. He was a short, scrawny man in Army uniform. He spared a glance at Kaden, then a second glance as he registered the lapel pin, which had Kaden examining it, himself. Symbol of the special flight team that was trained to land on battleships?

Holy Hydropod! Marshall could not hold back the choke that squeezed his throat. There was no way he'd be able to land on one of those. Short landings had been his failing in the Simulator Exercises. His SEN scores had been great, except for the fact that he needed an extra nine feet for landing.

The man bowed with a curt click of his boot heels. "Sir. Please forgive the interruption."

"What is it?"

He handed over an officially sealed and stamped missive. The President opened it.

Eleanor's head perked up with interest.

The President looked to her and grouched, "The Japanese Embassy is preparing to leave the city."

"Are you sure?"

"Absolute confirmation," the courier said.

"But, they haven't left yet?"

"No, Sir."

This was Kaden's opportunity to change history. All he had to do was tell the President that he had, somehow, learned that the Japanese had left because they were planning to bomb Pearl Harbor. But, a statement like that from a flyboy like him would land him under surveillance? And, if he were under surveillance, they'd go through his jacket's inner lining and how would he explain all that? Not to mention, the dead ringer he'd pushed through the portal. Kaden swallowed a lump in his throat. His head began to hurt.

He had to get this done and let the other man return before he missed out on copulation moments that might result in progeny. Eleanor cleared her throat and Kaden straightened in his chair. What was he doing letting his mind wander to sex in the Oval Office? That hadn't been allowed until the 1990's and the results had been scandalous.

Eleanor cleared her throat again. Franklin had gone still, staring at the missive. The courier fidgeted from one foot to the other waiting for a dismissal. Marshall felt the time was nearing to activate his last IDPP. Slowly, very slowly, he reached toward it.

The courier surprised him with a gun that came from nowhere and swung in his direction. "Hold it!"

He froze for a split second then smiled. He held up the gum pack. He rolled it in his fingers so that the label was easily visible.

"Relax," FDR said. "His clearance is higher than yours."

The courier, dutifully subdued, dejectedly holstered his weapon.

"I—I'm sorry," the courier said. "Is there a return message, Mr. President? If not, I'll take my leave."

"No. No return message. You may go."

"Do you mind?" Kaden had little choice but to put some gum in his mouth and chew. He even held it out, "Anybody?"

Relief washed through him as each one declined, the courier shaking his head as he exited the room. What would Sixta have thought if he'd gone and had FDR and his wife and some nobody courier chewing explosive gum? He slid the pack back into his jacket musing about what kind of message the President wanted him to deliver. In all his historical research he'd never encountered the account of an ancestor who had carried a special message from the President of the United States to someone else only hours before Pearl Harbor.

How on earth had that been buried? You'd have thought he'd mentioned it on his deathbed or something. In a journal, maybe. That would have been important enough to record, to zip, and chip, for future studiers of ancient civilization. There had to be an account of it somewhere otherwise Sixta would not have sent him.

But, which was the most important part? Convincing FDR to boost the forestry program? Or actually preventing the attack on Pearl Harbor?

Marshall knew what he needed to do. Leave some evidence for future generations, so they'd know to send someone back to this time and place—if his visit didn't work, and the cycle of history tampering had to be retried. But what?

He glanced around again at the antiquated office, eyeing the book on the table beside his chair. "Huh," he thought. Marshall had expected the place to look new. The books were a classic collection.

The President looked up.

"Mind if I look at one of your books? To hold something a president has held..."

Franklin waved, "Go ahead."

Lifting the closest one, Marshall opened it and slipped the gum wrapper into a page. Some future historian would find it, and analyze the paper, and... Yes, Kaden thought, it would be enough of a clue. He knew that minor clues of this nature had been left before, and worked as tips.

"I just wanted to say..." he rubbed a page between thumb and forefinger. "...I wish your forestry programs had been more successful."

Eleanor glanced up.

"I mean, we take for granted all the things that are around us, and..."

"One day they will be gone, if we don't do our part. I fully agree," Eleanor said. "Conservation is important."

Kaden chewed his gum, feeling it heat up with each chaw, its molecular chain structure changing with saliva and mixing. He slid it into his cheek. Better stop before it blew up in his mouth or something. Who had developed this particular product?

His mind went blank, which he supposed was a condition of the chemical reaction going on in his mouth. Powder residue poisoning wasn't dangerous, really. Marshall looked around for a trash receptacle. If he laid it in nice and neat....

Franklin threw a hand in the air after the departed courier. "It seems everybody wants to be a hero these days. Save the President." His voice took on an odd intonation. "Do I look like a moving target to you? If somebody wanted me dead, I'd be gone already."

"Security caught a man sneaking in through the kitchens last week, and he had a gun," Eleanor reminded him. "I've wanted to shoot you once or twice, myself. So, I wouldn't be so cocky, if I were you."

Franklin's lips curled in genuine amusement. He

winked at Kaden. "When a woman threatens you like that, you know they care."

"I guess."

Sixta could never, in a million light years duplicate the genuine, old-fashioned feel that Eleanor Roosevelt had about her. She blushed again and he realized he'd been staring. He smiled. The way she ducked her head was rather refreshing—since his experience with Sixta always meant direct eye contact. Flesh and blood women blushed and averted their gazes.

"I'm sure the Major is anxious to be on his way. There's a plane waiting for him, I bet."

"Yes. You're right." Franklin folded the missive he'd received and tapped it on his thigh, reminding Kaden a lot of Sixta.

Marshall had the good sense to swallow the extra saliva in his mouth before he choked on it. He was pretty sure he wasn't going to like whatever the President wanted him to do.

"What I want you to do is simple," FDR said. "You trained in Columbia Metropolitian Airport, right?"

Kaden had to rack his brain. Was this a test? Had something in his demeanor, or reaction to the courier, tipped the President off that he was an imposter? His mouth watered as he stared FDR in the eye.

"Yes. That's right." He nodded. "West Columbia, South Carolina.

With Doolittle."

"All right. I need to get a message to General Short, the Commander of the Hawaiian Army units. He sent me a message saying he believes that if Japan did attack, it would be somewhere in the southwest Pacific and not Pearl Harbor. All my other sources are saying we need to watch Wake and Midway Islands. I need him to deploy his task forces to those areas."

"But..." This didn't make sense. "Why ask me to carry the message?" He wanted to scream, I'm a pilot, not a courier! The guy who just left was more likely to be the man for the job.

FDR rolled his head as he said, "I can't trust anybody. Those Japs got taps on everything."

Kaden realized that this was a pivotal message for the war. If Short took his task force out of Pearl Harbor, it would be saved to fight the battles of Wake and Midway. And Short's ships weren't tied-in like those at Pearl. So, if Short's ships were deployed to Pearl Harbour instead to boost their defensive capabilities or if Pearl's ships were mobilized...

He opened his mouth to tell them when Eleanor abruptly put her knitting away and stood up.

"Five minutes of peace. That's all I wanted. I should have known this wasn't the place to come for it. You'll have to excuse me."

"What did I say?" FDR seemed confused for a second, wondering after Eleanor's change in mood. "Oh. Japs, probably."

While FDR was distracted by her abrupt departure, Kaden slipped the gum from his mouth, into his pocket.

"Women have some sensibilities I don't understand."

"You and me both."

The only woman he knew was Sixta. Kaden didn't have a clue as to how men handled the real thing.

Again, he thought seriously about popping the IDPP, but this time with the intention of announcing he was from the future and telling the President that he needed to believe his eyes and ears, and tell him, flat out, that there was an imminent attack on Pearl, and that he had to get his ships untied, and get on the horn to

Kimmel, and to seriously get after the forest preservation. No good to save the world from war now only to destroy it later by cutting down all the trees.

Wait a minute. He could fly to Pearl, get a bird's eye view, as they used to say, deliver the message to Short. Except, he'd have to land on a carrier.

Tick. Tick. Tick.

Another inkling slipped through Kaden's brain. Something he couldn't hold back.

"Uh, I have to ask you something, while I have your ear—if you don't mind, of course."

"What is that?"

"Why didn't you sign the Anti-Commintern Pact, the anti-Communist treaty signed by Germany, Italy and Japan in 1936/1937? We could have avoided this situation altogether, don't you think?"

FDR gave him the oddest look. His brows furrowed, his lids narrowed, and his lips pursed.

"And when you met with that Russian, Maxim Litvinov, on November 16, back in 1933, invited him here, even, and agreed to set up Soviet consulates on U.S. soil. I have to tell you that got my no vote. You legitimized communism.

Why did you do that? Can't you see, by your own policies, you've put the wheels in motion that started the great communist machine that has been warring against democracy for two years?"

The President's jaw dropped open. "Who *are* you?"

Kaden stood up. "Not the man that's going to deliver your message to Short. That'll have to go by another courier, or through regular channels. I'm from the future and I've come to give you a message."

FDR was speechless, but not for long. "Guard!"

"You need to hear what I have to say." Kaden reached in his coat and snatched the IDPP, popping it in his mouth, squirreling it over to his cheek. In an echo-sec, he also thumbed a grenade coin and whispered, "Grenade," flashing the inside of his jacket with all the gadgets intact.

The guards burst in. "Is everything all right, Sir?"

FDR caught sight of the tool supply in his jacket, and eyed the thing in his hand, swallowing hard, before he let his gaze go back to Marshall's face. Their eyes met. He held up a hand at the guards and smiled.

"Yes," Franklin finally said. "It's fine. Just keeping you on your toes, boys. Thanks for coming."

The guards looked around the room and withdrew. The door's discreet closing had Marshall turning his head to make sure it had, indeed, been drawn-to.

"All right. What do you want?"

"A couple answers and to tell you about what's gonna happen." Marshall gave the President his full attention.

"I don't believe you're from the future."

"I don't believe you want to ignore this." He held the coin up. "I can assure you, Mr. President. This *is* a grenade."

"Looks like a coin to me."

Kaden rolled his eyes. "That's the point. In the future, spies can waltz in and..."

"Prove you're from the future."

Had he just called himself a spy? What he should say is, in the future, Earth is a burnt out planet and that, sadly, your efforts at setting up Forestry Programs in 1929 and 1937 weren't enough, but if they'd been continued and expanded...

"I'm waiting. Surely, it can't be too hard to prove."

Kaden's brain snapped back to the here and now.

Well, he could toss the coin, or the gum, or a pellet bomb, but those would all be messy. He could write with his fancy ink pen, and keep the President hostage for an hour until he could see it fade, or...open a portal.

Sixta had to be waiting with other scientists to push that man and woman back to their "real time." Just opening the portal, and seeing them come through would probably be enough to convince the President. But, that would limit his talking time.

"I'll show you something in a minute, but just hear me out."

Franklin slapped his leg. "Does it look like I'm running off?"

"No, but...okay. This is...just listen...I'm here to stop Earth's forests from being destroyed and..." he caught his breath, "an attack on Pearl Harbor."

That got no reaction.

"You know you can't trust the Japanese. Tomorrow, while you're having lunch with your friend, you're going to get a message. Harry Hopkins is going to try and talk you out of believing it and he'll accomplish it, if you don't listen to me."

"I'm listening."

"You have to make some hard choices. Right now, the battleships in Pearl Harbor are tied together. If you don't get them untied and afloat, they are gonna be dead ducks."

"How do you know this information? I checked you out before I sent for you. You haven't been to Pearl yet."

"That's what I'm telling you. I know a lot of things about you."

"Tell me something other people don't know, then."

"You cheated on Eleanor with Lucy Page Mercer, her secretary, back in—"

"Something else."

"Um..." The pill in his cheek got swapped to the other side. "You collect stamps. Mark Twain's your favorite writer. He gestured toward the book he'd picked up. You like model ship building and you worked on a script on the history of the ship Old Ironsides when you were recovering from...you know."

Tired of talking, Kaden bit and spat. The portal appeared, the man and woman were thrust through, and Marshall said, "Just remember what I said. And, uh, these people are innocent. Brains are wiped. Aliens *do* exist."

He yanked the papers out of his coat and dropped them, then stepped through. Prismatic colors slid by once again, and on the other side, Sixta caught him by the sides of his jacket the minute he made the transition. She planted a big wet kiss on him, and said, "You're magnificent. Your MCR is gonna be so good."

As she tossed him down, he realized that there was no dome over their heads. High trees canopied above emitted pure oxygen...and she was naked

The End

About the author: Jennifer DiCamillo, President of Missouri Poets and Friends 2005 and 2006, has won over one hundred writing awards in the last three years, including the publishing contract for her first collection—out of an international field of 1500 poets. That is titled Passing Thoughts. Her works have appeared in: Grist, Museletter, The Poisoned Pen, Ozarks Magazine, Storyteller Magazine (US), Stride Magazine (UK), Taj Mahal Review (India), The Binnacle (University of Maine Press), True Confessions (Dorchester) and Cup of Comfort for Women in Love (Adams Media, US).

Her debut novel, The Price of Peace, won a CAPA nomination for Best Historical Fiction 2004. She looks forward to the release of her second award-winning novel, Courting Disaster (Zumaya Publications), as well as her paranormal mystery anthology with CJ Winters, Deadknots (Hard Shell Word Factory), and another mystery anthology, Despicado (Under the Moon Press). She has recently signed a contract with Rain Publishing Inc. of Canada for her second poetry collection, Passing Images.